D0909131

THE
SECRET
CIRCLE
The Temptation

The Vampire Diaries novels

VOL. I: THE AWAKENING

VOL. II: THE STRUGGLE

VOL. III: THE FURY

VOL. IV: DARK REUNION

THE RETURN VOL. I: NIGHTFALL

THE RETURN VOL. 2: SHADOW SOULS

THE RETURN VOL. 3: MIDNIGHT

THE HUNTERS VOL. I: PHANTOM

THE HUNTERS VOL. 2: MOONSONG

THE HUNTERS VOL. 3: DESTINY RISING

The Stefan's Diaries novels

VOL. I: ORIGINS

VOL. 2: BLOODLUST

VOL. 3: THE CRAVING

VOL. 4: THE RIPPER

VOL. 5: THE ASYLUM

VOL. 6: THE COMPELLED

The Secret Circle novels

THE INITIATION AND THE CAPTIVE PART I

THE CAPTIVE PART II AND THE POWER

THE DIVIDE

THE HUNT

Created by

L. J. SMITH

Written by Aubrey Clark

THE SECRET CIRCLE

The Temptation

HARPER TEEN
An Imprint of HarperCollins*Publishers*

HarperTeen is an imprint of HarperCollins Publishers.

The Secret Circle: The Temptation
www.epicreads.com

alloy**entertainment**
Produced by Alloy Entertainment
151 West 26th Street
New York, NY 10001
www.alloyentertainment.com

Library of Congress catalog card number: 2012955883
ISBN 978-0-06-213047-1 (trade bdg.)
ISBN 978-0-06-220596-4 (int. ed.)

Typography by Liz Dresner
13   14   15   16   17   CG/RRDH   10 9 8 7 6 5 4 3 2 1
❖
First Edition

THE
SECRET
CIRCLE
The Temptation

CHAPTER 1

It was a cool, purple night, and the candles continued to burn, flickering orange and yellow against the cave walls. But the hunters no longer mumbled their soft chant. They'd fallen silent. Their hardened bodies littered the ground, with their faces frozen in a soundless eternal scream.

Cassie looked at her hands, dirty and shaking. What had she done?

She glanced at Adam. He appeared pale and sickened, unsteady on his feet like he might faint.

Diana seemed a little dazed, unable to figure out what had just occurred.

The smell of death was thick in the air. As Cassie

breathed it in, her mouth filled with the heady, metallic taste of guilt.

Then Max's voice boomed. "You just killed my father. He's dead! Do you understand that?"

Slowly, Cassie's friends surrounded her, but they were no longer themselves—their faces had altered into distorted and ugly shapes. Adam sneered with narrowed blackened eyes and spoke in a voice that wasn't his own. "Give us the book, dear one," he said. "Or die."

Diana curled her fingers and twitched. "Better yet," she said, "give us the book and then die."

So much death, Cassie thought. *When will it stop?* Fear coursed through her.

She tried to back away, but she found herself pinned against the rocky wall of the cave. There was nowhere to run.

Melanie reached out and grabbed Cassie by the neck. She squeezed her long fingers tight around Cassie's throat, cutting off her breath.

Laurel clapped and cheered in a piercing, morbid singsong: "Die, die, die!"

I'm not ready to die! Cassie tried to scream.

But she couldn't find her voice, and she couldn't breathe, and soon the flickering cave walls went black—

She startled awake, gasping for air.

Cassie looked around her dark bedroom, confused about where she was. She mentally rifled through the last twenty-four hours, separating what was real from what she'd just imagined. The truth gradually snaked itself around her guts.

Her nightmare was her reality.

That evening at the caves, after performing the curse that destroyed the witch-hunters, the boy she loved and all her closest friends had turned into monsters before her eyes. The truth of it pierced her chest like a slick blade and remained there, stuck—there was no release.

The alarm clock on her nightstand told her it was almost morning, but the sky through her window was clouded over in charcoal gray. A storm must be coming. She reached over to the lamp's hanging beaded cord and tugged it to life. Scattered around her bedroom floor, Cassie saw pages and pages of her handwriting—translations, notes, doodles—all scribbled the previous night while she worked through Black John's Book of Shadows. She'd fallen asleep trying to figure out a way to save her possessed friends.

Now, beneath the soft yellow glow of her lamp, Cassie reexamined what she'd written on each page. She'd translated reams of dark magic spells and incantations, but, so far, she'd had no luck finding a single word referring to demon possession.

Cassie picked up her father's Book of Shadows from where it lay on the floor. She rested it upon her lap and stared at its aged cover. It looked like any old book, but she knew the power contained in its pages. Opening it didn't burn her fingers anymore, the way it once did. Because it was a part of her now, and she was a part of it—for better or worse.

A crack of thunder caused Cassie to flinch. Then the sky opened, unleashing a violent rain against the glass of her windows.

She blushed at her own jumpiness. Her spell had trapped her friends in the cave, Cassie reminded herself, so at least for now, she was safe. However, running her fingers through the book's tattered pages, Cassie reflected that *safe* was hardly how she'd describe what she felt at the moment. *Determined* was more like it.

Cassie awoke for the second time that morning to a room that was sunny and bright. She climbed out of bed, thankful the storm had passed, and went to her window to greet the ocean. Admiring the way it rolled and sparkled never ceased to calm her—but today the beach struck her as lonesome, abandoned. No person could be seen for miles.

Cassie dressed quickly and went downstairs to find her mom making enough pancakes to feed an army.

"Oh, no," she said aloud.

Her mother looked up from the sizzling butter in her frying pan. "What's wrong?"

"Everything," Cassie said. "But for the moment, there's the small problem that no one's here to eat these."

Cassie picked a pancake from the top of a pile, rolled it in her hands, and bit into it like a piece of licorice. Sitting down at the kitchen table, she tried to figure out the best way to explain the events of last night to her mother. But there was no best way. She just had to come out with it straight: They'd gone to the caves, performed the hunter curse, and Scarlett betrayed them.

"The hunters died," Cassie said, still hardly able to believe it herself. "The spell killed them all, even Max's dad."

Her mother's naturally pale skin appeared to whiten. She pitched forward, ignoring the pancake currently sizzling and smoking in the pan, and motioned Cassie to continue.

"Now the whole Circle is possessed. To perform the curse, we had to call upon Black John's ancestors, and they've taken hold of everyone and won't let go. I've been poring through Black John's book trying to find a way to save them, but I haven't been able to find anything remotely helpful."

"I told you to leave that book alone." Her mother's voice sounded severe, like a scolding. She turned off the stove and abandoned her pancake batter, then reached for a dish towel and wiped off her hands. She was quiet for a few seconds, twisting the towel sorrowfully in her fingers.

Cassie knew she should have listened about not touching her father's book. Maybe her mother thought she'd gotten what she deserved.

But when she finally looked up, the only emotion on her mother's face was concern. "Is it awful that all I can think right now is how happy I am that you're okay?" she said. Her long dark hair framed her face like a shroud.

"That's one way of looking at it," Cassie said, but the look she gave her mom betrayed her true concern.

"Possession is serious, Cassie. If there's a way to save your friends, it won't come easy, and you surely can't do it alone."

Cassie's heart sank like a heavy stone.

An odd expression crossed her mother's face, a flash of discomfort, of pain. "There's a man," she said. "On the mainland. In Concord. He used to live in New Salem a long time ago."

Cassie waited for her mother to say more, but she didn't.

"Who is he?" As far as Cassie knew, her mother had broken ties with everyone from her past days in New Salem.

"Last I heard, he was the head librarian at a research institute that specializes in the occult." Her mother began cleaning up—something she always did when she was ill at ease. "He may know something."

"Why haven't you ever mentioned him before?" Cassie asked.

Her mother averted her eyes. "We didn't exactly part on the best of terms."

"But you think he can help?"

"If there's a man alive who knows how to perform an exorcism, it's him."

Exorcism, Cassie thought. Just the word brought a shiver to her spine. She imagined heads whirling around like spinning tops, projectile vomiting. Was that what was in store for the people she loved most?

"He's a scholar, an academic," her mother said. "Not a priest or anything like that. His name is Timothy Dent."

She focused on the task of collecting the broken egg-shells from the countertop and dropping them into the trash. "We should go see him right away. The more time that passes, the worse it'll be for your friends."

Cassie took a sip of her mother's cup of coffee and found that it had already become cold.

"Have a little more to eat." Her mother placed a plate of pancakes and a bottle of maple syrup on the table in front of Cassie and handed her a fork and knife. "You can't help anyone else if you don't take care of yourself first."

Cassie nodded, but the last person she was thinking of right now was herself.

CHAPTER 2

Cassie's mother waited in the car while Cassie ran inside the Cup for two to-go cappuccinos and some biscotti for the road. She opened the door to the coffee shop with a shakiness she couldn't name—part exhaustion, part dread. Why was her mother so tight-lipped about this man they were going to see? Her stomach felt too queasy for biscotti.

Once inside the shop, she inhaled a deep breath of coffee-scented air and tried to steer her feelings toward hope. The Cup was crowded as usual, which gave her a few minutes to collect herself. She observed the line of people waiting at the counter: a twenty-something girl yapping on her cell phone, a taller, older woman deliberating over apple or strawberry rhubarb pie. Then Cassie spotted broad shoulders beneath a black T-shirt that she recognized instantly—Max. Her breath caught in her throat.

With everything that had happened, it was hard for Cassie to believe that only a few hours before she'd seen Max at the caves, where he'd watched his fellow hunters fall dead at the hands of the Circle. Cassie knew she would never be able to forget the way Max passed his eyes over each member of the Circle as his father breathed his last breath in his arms. How he'd glared at Diana, threatening her not to follow him, before running from the cave and disappearing into the night.

As if sensing her gaze, Max turned around and locked eyes with Cassie. He froze, his face reddened, and then he quickly ducked off line and headed for the exit.

"Max, wait," Cassie called out, chasing after him without knowing what she would actually say if she caught him.

Max stormed through the bodies obstructing his way toward the door, trying to make a quick escape. In his haste, he bumped into a double-seat baby carriage. It was just the holdup Cassie needed. She reached out and caught him by the bicep.

"Please," she said, hoping Max would see how sorry she was.

He aggressively shook off her hold, drawing the attention of everyone on line. "You're the last person I want to see," he said.

"I know that." Cassie took a step back and lowered her voice to a whisper. The whole coffee shop seemed to fall silent. "None of us knew that was going to happen. I know that doesn't change anything, but . . ."

Max scowled and looked away. Through clenched teeth he said, "My father's body isn't even cold yet. Have a little respect." His eyes welled up.

Cassie registered the intense look of pain on Max's face and felt it as her own. It must have been what her face looked like after Suzan died—that unmovable mask that Cassie thought was strong but still betrayed her true feelings.

There was nothing Cassie could say to ease Max's pain. None of what had happened could be undone.

"I trusted Diana," Max said. "And I trusted you, too. Now my dad's gone. Please, just don't make it any worse."

He broke from Cassie's hold, and she knew he was right. Trying to explain away what the Circle had done, or to bring Max further into the drama, wasn't fair. This was his opportunity for a clean break, to not be part of this life anymore.

Cassie nodded to Max, an almost imperceptible agreement to everything he'd said. He rushed for the exit, shoulder and hip checking everyone and everything standing in his way, but when he reached the door he turned back around. His eyes locked with Cassie's.

Was he having second thoughts? Did he consider hearing Cassie out? She waited for him to say something, anything.

He hesitated for only a few seconds before breaking his gaze and continuing through the door.

Cassie watched him go. She'd felt alone before, but now she felt . . . There weren't even words for it.

"Are you okay, miss?" the manager behind the counter asked. He frowned sympathetically at Cassie, as if she was the victim of a hot-tempered boyfriend.

"I'm fine, thank you," Cassie said, though she wasn't fine at all. She rushed to order and escape the customers' pitying stares. She couldn't get out of there fast enough.

Cassie and her mother's road trip destination was Concord, Massachusetts, a town made famous by some of Cassie's favorite authors—Louisa May Alcott, Nathaniel Hawthorne, Henry David Thoreau.

"It's so pretty here," Cassie said. "I wish we could actually explore it." She soaked in the flowering oaks, leafy elms, and red and black maples. It was no wonder all those writers found inspiration here.

"We're getting close. Hopefully we'll have some good news soon," her mother replied. Her thumb had begun rubbing back and forth upon the leather of the steering wheel as she drove—a telling nervous tic. She wasn't offering much in the way of conversation.

Cassie tried to focus on the colonial architecture and bucolic country roads, but the suspense was killing her.

"So why this librarian? What can you tell me about him?" she asked.

Her mother took off her sunglasses, propped them up on the top of her head, and looked straight ahead. "You'll meet him for yourself soon enough," she said.

"But how do you know him?"

"He used to know your grandmother. He's an elder, a bit of an eccentric."

Cassie noticed her mother's grip tighten more securely around the steering wheel.

"What aren't you telling me?" Cassie asked.

Her mother forced a smile. She watched the winding, barely paved road stretched out before them.

"Timothy Dent had a falling out with John Blake sixteen years ago," she said.

Cassie knew there had to be more. She waited for it, and after a few more seconds, her mother added, "As a result, he was stripped of his power and banished from New Salem."

"So they were enemies," Cassie said. "He and my father. What were they fighting over?"

"By the end they were fighting about everything," her mother said. "Timothy was extremely powerful back then. But he wasn't a Crowhaven witch. He wasn't a part of any Circle. Which was why your father did to him what he did."

"But he was friends with Grandma Howard," Cassie said.

"You have to understand, Cassie, it was a crazy time. People started breaking up into factions. Friends became enemies, former enemies became allies. Everyone was fighting with someone."

"About dark magic?" Cassie asked. "Is that what all the fighting was about?"

But her mother didn't respond to that question,

perhaps because the _____ et's just
say Timothy may not _____

   She put her sunglasse_____ driving
in silence.

CHAPTER 3

The library was on an unmarked road set back on a long stretch of rocky, barren land. The two-story building's gray facade of crumbly mortar slanted slightly forward as if it were taking a bow. Cassie could barely make out the wording etched across a sign hanging over the door: THE TIMOTHY DENT LIBRARY OF THE OCCULT.

Cassie stepped out of the car first, and then her mother followed suit. They stood side by side for a few seconds taking it all in before moving forward. By the looks of the building's exterior, Cassie thought they might have come all this way for nothing. The library seemed empty, possibly even abandoned. But her mother assured her that

Timothy would be in there, quite possibly alone, but there.

They pushed open a heavy wooden door and stepped inside.

It took a few seconds for Cassie's eyes to adjust from the bright sunlight to the dimly lit foyer lined with tall wooden bookcases. The floor was a checkerboard of stone-gray squares that led to a high brown counter. Standing behind it was a small man leaning over a massive manuscript. He didn't look up.

Cassie's mother led Cassie toward the counter. "That's him," she whispered.

As they stepped closer, the man came into focus. Cassie could see his wrinkles and the raised freckle on the side of his face. Dust streaked his black short-sleeved dress shirt, and his fingernails were yellow. Still with his eyes on the tome before him, he spoke in a gravelly voice. "Alexandra."

Cassie's mother remained quiet until he finally looked up. His eyes matched the gray of the floor tile.

"After all these years, you show up here like this without warning," he said. "I can only imagine the horrors that have driven you here. Too bad I don't care."

The gravel of his voice shot across the foyer, ricocheting between the rickety columns lining the perimeter of the room like soldiers. Cassie realized she was holding her breath.

Her mother stepped forward in spite of Timothy's rebuke, and Cassie had the urge to pull her back.

"You're right, we are in trouble," her mother said in a barely audible tone. "Please just hear me out."

"It's exhausting, being right about everything." Timothy shut his book and stared at Cassie's mother with a curious expression.

"This is my daughter Cassie," her mother said.

Timothy squinted his eyes and turned slowly to get a better look at Cassie. The sensation was similar to being on stage, under a glaring spotlight.

"Black John's daughter, you mean," he said. "You poor, poor thing." But it wasn't sympathy he was actually offering her; it was pity. It was a condolence.

Timothy tottered around the counter. Only then did Cassie recognize how frail his body was.

"You." He pointed a dirty fingernail at Cassie's mother. "Come no further. I don't trust your motives."

He turned again to look at Cassie while continuing to address her mother. "This victim of your foolishness and that evil man's darkness can come with me."

He made his way toward a set of glass doors, which

Cassie understood to be his office, without bothering to check if she was following him.

She made no motion to until her mother gave her a sharp nudge. "Go," she said. "Don't let him scare you. Listen carefully to what he has to say."

Cassie obeyed and followed Timothy into his office. He closed the glass doors behind him and gestured for her to sit on the orange vinyl chair opposite his desk. Hesitantly, she settled into the chair.

The office was much like the rest of the library: dusty, pulpy, and a little creepy. The wall behind Timothy's desk was a row of dark cabinets protected by chunky brass padlocks. He unlocked one of them and retrieved an oversized book, thick with plastic-covered pages.

"Have you always known what you are?" he asked, dropping the tanned leather book onto the desk in front of her.

What, not *who* you are.

"No," Cassie said, looking at the book. Branded onto its cover were the letters B-L-A-K.

"I worked closely with your grandmother, you know," Timothy said. "To try to save your mother from that awful man. But their bond had been too strong. She was a lost cause."

"I'm not sure if you heard," Cassie said. "But my grand-mother passed away earlier this year."

Timothy's face wrinkled forlornly. He sat down. "Oh," he said, looking at his hands. "No, I hadn't heard."

Cassie watched his reaction. He'd softened before her eyes.

"She was an amazing woman," he said. "But I'm sure you know that."

Cassie nodded.

"She and I joined forces against your father," Timothy continued. "We knew that awful man would play your mother for a fool. But she was charmed by him the way everyone else was. I'll never forget the way your grand-mother cried on my shoulder the day John Blake betrayed your mother."

Timothy touched his bony fingers to his shoulder as if Cassie's grandmother's tears might still be damp on his shirt. "She was devastated when your mother left New Salem. Not a day went by that she didn't wonder about you, Cassie, the granddaughter she never knew."

Cassie felt a knot form in her throat. She'd gotten so little time with her grandmother before she died. If only she could have known her as well as Timothy had.

"But I suspect you've dropped in on me today for a

more pressing reason," Timothy said, "than to reminisce about the past."

"Yes." Cassie's voice sounded meek to her own ears. "My Circle performed a dark-magic spell from my father's Book of Shadows. A witch-hunter curse that left them possessed by . . ." She trailed off.

"By evil spirits?" Timothy asked.

Cassie looked down at a stain on the floor, an amoeba of coffee or soda that had never been properly scrubbed clean.

"Your ancestors," Timothy said.

For some reason, relief settled into Cassie's shoulders. This man might be a little strange, but he seemed to understand. "How did you know?" she asked.

Timothy pointed to the leather book he'd dropped onto the desk. "I've studied the Blak family—that's the Middle English spelling of *Black* without the 'c'—for decades. All dark magic can be traced back to the early days of the Blak family."

All dark magic, Cassie thought. That was practically like saying *all evil in the world* had originated from her ancestors. She was beginning to understand why her mother had kept her from this man for so long. He had nothing good to tell her.

"I a ... the Black Death in school? ... plague?"

"Ye ... she really recall? Some rats, t ... sick and dying. She hadn't ...

"Yo ... ory," Timothy said. "Medie ... atastrophe many different ... or the Great Plague. It wasn ... started describing the ev ...

Tim ... sink in. "Historians today a ... refers to *black* in the sense ... the events, as well as the ... skin to turn black with gangre ... that by the fifteenth century pe ... was really going on."

"W ... asked.

"A ... the name of Blak were w ... Timothy said. "They hated ... them, and they had no qu ...

C ... was my family?"

Ti ... c-minded argued that th ... rats and their fleas.

That was true—but the rats had been bespelled by your ancestors. It took years, as the death tolls rose and hysteria grew, for more and more people to believe there was a supernatural cause for the sickness. That sinister witches were at fault."

Cassie's legs felt weak even though she was sitting down.

"It was a terrible time for witches and warlocks who weren't of the Blak bloodline," Timothy continued. "There were persecutions and massacres. But the real witches responsible, the Blaks, were smarter and much more powerful than the thousands of innocent witches who were persecuted."

"But what started it all?" Cassie asked. "What did the Blaks want?"

Timothy grinned. "That's the mystery I've been trying to solve for more than thirty years."

"And?" Cassie asked. "Have you found the answer?"

"It seems that very early on, the man who began your family's Book of Shadows was determined to attain eternal life. He made a deal with the devil. Sold his soul in order to live forever, but it backfired. When he died, his bloodline was cursed. And so was his book."

"Cursed," Cassie repeated.

Timothy allowed her a few seconds to process this new knowledge. "You come from a line of ancestors cursed with black magic, and all the uncontrollable urges that come with it."

"I'm bound to my father's book," she said. "I wasn't possessed like the rest of my friends because I've got his blood in my veins. So I must really be one of them. Is what you're telling me, that I'm destined to be evil, too?"

Timothy shook his head. "You're an innocent child. You can't help what you come from. You can only control what you do with it—though it may not always be so easy for you to control."

Timothy turned his attention to the leather album on his desk. "The Book of Shadows you're bound to was composed over centuries and passed down through the Blak family, from the people I've just told you about, all the way to the Salem witch trials, where Black John's younger sister fell victim to the inquisitions, and finally to Black John when he reappeared in New Salem as John Blake. That's how the book ended up in your mother's hands, I imagine."

Cassie had gotten stuck midway through Timothy's explanation. *Black John had a sister?* It wasn't such a far-fetched idea, just not one Cassie had ever considered.

Did that mean Cassie had other family out there besides Scarlett?

"What was she like?" Cassie asked. "Black John's sister."

Timothy flipped through the leather album. When he found the page he was searching for, he turned it around for Cassie to view close up. It was an artistic rendering, a drawing of a girl just around Cassie's age.

"This was Alice Black," Timothy said. "She was hanged in 1693."

Cassie stared down at the drawing, which was so detailed it looked like a black-and-white photograph. Alice's hair was pulled tightly back in some sort of bun or braid. Her face was thin and slight, nearly lost within the lofty height of her collar. But it was her expression that was the most striking. She wasn't pouting, but her lips protruded just so, into a natural sulk. And her eyes— though it was just a rendering, Cassie could feel Alice's cavernous eyes watching her. They were filled with long- ing and sadness. No, not sadness, Cassie realized. Anger. Anger directed outward, for sure, but also turned brutally in on herself.

Timothy continued talking before Cassie could fully digest the tragic face of her young aunt. "These spirits possessing your Circle," he said, "are the souls of your ancestors that managed to return when your father's spell was channeled. Only the strongest would have gotten through."

"But Alice was so young, and so beautiful," Cassie said, nearly to herself.

Timothy shut the book to fully regain Cassie's attention. "That girl there was one of the most nefarious of them all. Don't be fooled by her looks. Some say she was more evil than Black John himself."

Cassie wanted to reopen the album and look at the picture again, but she knew she had to focus on why she'd come to see Timothy in the first place. "What can I do to save my friends from these spirits?" she asked. "Is there a way?"

"There should be an exorcism spell in your father's Book of Shadows," Timothy said. "From one of your ancestors from the sixteenth century."

Timothy opened the album again and turned to a different plastic-covered page. "This man." He pointed to another drawing, more sparse and faded than the other. It was a sketch of faded lines, barely recognizable as a face.

"Absolom Blak," Timothy said. "He lived his life as a priest but corrupted the Church. He was rumored to have copied the forbidden text of the exorcism rite into his own book. The Book of Shadows that later became your father's."

Cassie couldn't stomach the thought that the dark soul of this evil priest could right now be in the body of one of her closest friends. It nauseated her so much she had to turn away.

"The exorcism is the spell you have to find," Timothy said. "But it might be dangerous. Absolom was an evil man who would have only copied the exorcism rite for wicked reasons. He may have doctored the text, changed things. And that could have consequences. But you *must* find it, Cassie. It's a risk you'll have to take. You'll be shocked to see how quickly these evil spirits will adapt to your friends' bodies and to the modern world. You don't have much time."

"What am I even looking for?" Cassie asked. "How will I know when I find it?"

"Absolom was definitely the one to add it to the book," Timothy said. "So try to figure out which sections he might have contributed to."

He turned to another page of the album. "Here's another ancestor you should keep your eye out for. Another one who died young, like Alice."

Timothy directed Cassie's attention to a faded black-and-white pamphlet or what may have been a cutout of an old newspaper drawing. It was so frayed and soft at its edges it looked almost like felt. Cassie had to strain her eyes to make out its image.

It was a picture of a persecution, not of one person but many.

"It's a witch trial," Timothy said.

The writing beneath the picture was in German, and a barely legible caption stated the year: 1594.

"Beatrix Blak was burned alive in the Trier massacre," Timothy said. "The charge was sorcery. They say her last words were 'You haven't seen the last of me.' So you can be sure she's one of the spirits who made it back—and is currently ravaging the insides of one of your friends."

Timothy shut the book again and pushed it toward Cassie. "Take it home with you," he said. "Study it."

Cassie took the book into her lap.

"You must be very careful," Timothy continued. "These spirits will try to trick you. Some of your friends might appear normal at times, like their regular selves, but don't be fooled. The only way you'll be able to tell if they're possessed or not is by their heartbeats. Hearts can't lie. The heart of a possessed body will beat four times faster than a regular heart. Remember that."

"So it is possible then," Cassie said. "For some of them to break through the possession."

"Possible, but not likely." Timothy's eyebrows crumpled sadly over his eyes. "Pretty soon, Cassie, these friends of yours will be long gone. If the possession lasts until the next full moon, it'll become permanent."

"Permanent?" Cassie felt her face flush. "But the next full moon is less than two weeks away."

"I told you," Timothy said. "You don't have much time."

The sinking feeling in Cassie's stomach dropped to a new low. This was a bad idea; she wasn't strong enough to hear any more.

"I have to go," she said, and stood up abruptly. "Thank you for your help."

She turned toward the door, but Timothy grabbed her firmly on the wrist and pulled her back down to her seat. "Wait," he said. "One last thing."

His hand felt warm on her skin. She'd expected it to be cold, like his eyes.

"I'm a simple man," he said. "A lonely, powerless man. Forgive me if I frighten you."

He was still holding Cassie's wrist. "But in you, I can see light," he said.

Timothy gradually released his hold once he was sure Cassie wouldn't run away. He stared deep into her eyes.

"The strength inside you," he said. "And the love you have for your friends. That love can be the most powerful spell of all."

Cassie wasn't sure how to respond, or if she should respond at all.

"Do you understand?" he asked.

"I think so." Cassie nodded hesitantly at first, then with more assurance. "Yes."

Timothy came around his desk and opened his office door to the foyer. "Then there's nothing else you need but luck."

With the album tucked beneath her arm, Cassie ran back out to the library's main room, though she wasn't sure why she was running. Timothy was strange, but she didn't think he was harmful. In a way, she felt sorry for him.

As Cassie rejoined her mother in the car, she couldn't get Timothy's last few words out of her head—that love was more powerful than all of this.

Silently, Cassie began to forge a plan. She needed to

visit Adam in the cave. If Timothy was right about the power of love, maybe Cassie could break through to Adam after all. Whose love was stronger than theirs? And who better to help her search for the exorcism spell than Adam?

Cassie was calmed by this thought. In her mind it was decided. She would bring Adam through tonight, and together they would save the rest of their friends.

CHAPTER 4

*The caves felt frigid in the dark of night even though the tem-*perature hovered around a balmy eighty degrees. Cassie found herself shivering as she rowed the final few feet to land. She wasn't sure what to expect traveling here alone. In her imagination the whole angry mob of her friends would be waiting for her, salivating, hungry to return the pain she'd caused them by trapping them there.

Dry-mouthed, she brought in her oars and awaited the worst. She was relieved to see there was only one person visible at the mouth of the cave. A dark shadow of the tall, strong body she knew well. Adam. He was sitting out near the exit, hugging his knees toward his chest, looking lonely. The others must have been deeper within the cave, sleeping.

Cassie beached her rowboat and moved toward Adam with careful determination. Her heart knocked against her ribs as she took quiet steps, one foot in front of the other, until she stood before him—just out of his reach beyond the barrier in the cave. At first she said nothing, just watched him, and tried to locate the *real* him somewhere inside this shell of the boy she loved.

"Cassie," he said, sounding just like his true self. He stood up with joy. "I was just watching the water wishing you would appear, and now here you are."

He looked good, she thought. A little dirty, but aside from that nothing about him appeared different. His hair still shone with multicolored streaks of auburn in the moonlight, and his eyes were their natural, gorgeous blue. There was a vulnerability to their depth that couldn't be feigned.

"How do you feel?" she asked.

"Better now that you're here." Adam reached out his hand, but it couldn't pass through the bound cave entrance. "If only I could touch you," he said, frowning.

Cassie was careful not to get too close. "How do I know it's really you?" she asked. "And not the demon."

Adam reached out his hand again, this time open palmed with his fingers outstretched. "It's me," he said. "I swear. Let me prove it to you. Raise up your hand to mine."

The binding spell Cassie had cast on the cave trapped all witches inside. If she entered the cave, she wouldn't be able to come back out. But she could simply meet Adam's hand like he'd asked her to.

She watched his eyes. There was nothing strange or distorted about them.

"I can't," Cassie said, though she wanted to.

"Just meet my fingertips. You'll still be safe." He poked at the invisible border, causing it to sizzle against his skin. "See? I can't reach through."

The truth was, Cassie longed for Adam's touch, even if he was still possessed. It would be worth it to feel him for only a second and then pull her hand away.

"Our bond is stronger than all of this," Adam said. "Not even a demon can break it." He stretched his fingers toward Cassie again. "Believe me."

Only for a second, Cassie thought, as she slowly raised her hand. That was all she'd allow herself. She guided her fingers to Adam's, precisely at the border between the inside of the cave and out.

The sensation was electric. From her fingertips, down her spine, all the way to her feet, sparks fired. Her skin tingled. It felt like the first time she ever performed magic.

She looked at the meeting point between her hand and Adam's, where the silver cord manifested and hummed. It wrapped itself around them, entwining their arms, their entire bodies, in a band of light.

That was all the convincing Cassie needed. Adam was still in there, and she was sure this was him with her now. The cord binding them heart to heart, drawing them closer, didn't lie. It *couldn't* lie.

Adam made no attempt to grasp Cassie's wrist or pull her toward him, none of the things he could easily have done to overpower her if he'd been possessed by an evil demon. He simply enjoyed the sensation of the tips of his fingers joining hers and the cord reinforcing their bond.

Cassie thought back to what Timothy had said, that love was the strongest of all magic. That's what she felt coursing through her veins now—love. And Adam's love for her was so strong that it was proving to be more powerful than the demon battling for his body.

"I want to hold you," Adam said. "I need to."

Cassie brought her hand back down to her side. "But if I let you out, the others will also be free."

"Together we can handle them, Cassie. There's no telling what they'll do to me if I'm stuck in here and they figure out I'm not one of them. Why do you think I've been sitting here, as far away from them as possible?"

Cassie hadn't thought of that. Adam could be in danger if she left him here another night. She'd never forgive herself if something happened to him.

And she was so lonely. So alone. How different this battle would be with Adam at her side. Why not set Adam free and then quickly recast the spell to keep the others in the cave?

"Okay," Cassie said. "Stand back."

Without another thought, she raised both her hands up and called out in her most commanding voice: "*Hoc captionem est levavi.*"

The rocky cave walls shuddered and shook. Cassie focused all her power on the cave's entrance until the containment spell she had cast there was broken.

Adam smiled and drew in a deep breath. He stepped forward to test his freedom.

Looking at him made Cassie dizzy. She couldn't take her eyes from his as she rushed into his outstretched arms.

Their embrace was all she'd hoped it would be and more. He held nothing back, kissing her mouth, her neck.

She closed her eyes to better enjoy him—the feel of his hair, the smell of his skin, the sound of his heavy breath in her ear. His heartbeat was fast—racing. Timothy's warning echoed in her mind.

She slipped from his embrace and took a step back. Even in the darkness she immediately noticed the change. First it showed itself in the bend of his lips, then the tilt of his head. The way he curled his fingers cruelly into his palms.

"Adam," she said, as if the familiar utterance of his name might keep him from turning on her. But then eel-like lesions formed on his forehead and face, and his eyes blackened.

"Oh, Cassie," he said in a voice generations more malevolent than his own. "You're such a sweet girl, but so easily duped."

Just like that, he wasn't her Adam at all. He was a many-faced monster, exactly like in her nightmare. Cassie was poised to recast the guarding spell on the cave, but with a flick of Adam's fingers her legs spilled out from under her.

CHAPTER 5

Diana appeared from the deep shadow of the cave, followed by Melanie and Laurel. Faye, Deborah, and the others were behind them. They were all still visibly possessed, but more subtly than before. The irises of their eyes were less noticeably etched in black, and the slithering lesions festering on their faces were less pronounced. But it was obvious to Cassie they weren't themselves.

Scarlett hung back in the shadows—the only one besides Cassie who was not possessed. Satisfied, she watched Cassie writhing on the ground, struggling to regain her strength.

"Did she bring us the book?" Melanie asked.

Diana twitched awkwardly. "Search her," she commanded.

Faye kneeled down, her mouth leering threateningly. Deborah crouched at Cassie's side and roughly patted her body up and down, frisking her for the book.

Cassie scanned all the faces hovering over her. Weak as she was, limp on the ground, she strove to decipher which ancestors had invaded her friends. If she paid close enough attention, she thought she might be able to recognize who some of them were, based on what Timothy had told her earlier that day. If they revealed themselves, maybe she could use it against them.

Deborah stood up and turned brusquely to the others. "No book," she said.

Sean and the Henderson brothers grimaced. Adam kicked a stone in frustration.

"Patience," Diana said. "We'll get it from her one way or another."

Scarlett wrapped her arm around Adam's waist and smiled down at Cassie. Her red hair was knotted and untamed, dusty from the cave. Adam drew her in and kissed her forehead. "It won't be long now," he said.

Cassie flinched. Adam and Scarlett? Were they . . . *together?*

Adam was holding her so close. He rubbed the small of her back with his thumb, and Cassie could sense their silver cord now, humming and connecting *them*. Even with Adam possessed, their cord remained.

It felt like Cassie had been knifed in the heart. She coughed, unsure if it was the spell Adam had cast or purely her heartbreak causing the twisting pain.

Diana crossed her thin arms over her chest. Cassie concentrated on her familiar cheekbones and her long golden hair, searching for any sign as to who inhabited her body. Could it be Black John's sister, Alice?

Cassie looked at Sean, slinking and beady-eyed, and then at Chris's and Doug's sharp-featured identical faces. She wondered if each ancestor chose its host for a reason. It would make sense, she thought, that the spirits would identify the most comfortable body for their invasion. But for the moment, none of the spirits were immediately recognizable.

Adam stepped forward and held his open hands— priest-like hands, Cassie thought—over her body. He stared down at her with his hard black eyes, and she grew weaker still. She could feel her life force draining from her veins, leaking out in a puddle beneath her body.

"Leave her, Absolom," Diana said. "This is a waste of your energy. We need to regain our strength."

Absolom?

"She's right." Scarlett pulled Adam back by the arm. "We're finally free. Let's get out of here." She turned to the group. "Follow me."

Diana and the others made their way to the boats behind her. In the darkness they appeared to vanish into thin air after only a few steps.

Faye called back to Cassie from the void. "Don't worry," she said in her husky voice, which was at once both foreign and familiar. "This won't be the last you see of us."

Those final words echoed inside the cave like a warning, ringing out with truth.

~~~~~~~~~

Still lying on the ground at the mouth of the cave, Cassie shook with fear. She looked around to be sure she was alone, that—for the moment at least—all the ancestors had gone.

But she wasn't alone. Someone stirred behind her and sluggishly said her name.

"Nick?" she said.

It hadn't occurred to Cassie that she didn't see him earlier; he must have been hanging back in the cave all along.

He stepped out into the moonlight and came into full view.

Weak and sweating, uneasy on his feet, he looked like he was suffering from the flu. "Don't be afraid," he said feebly. But Cassie could see the darkness in his eyes and the slithering things beneath the skin of his face.

With Diana and the others gone, Cassie felt her strength returning. She was able to climb up to a standing position and back away from Nick, watching him carefully.

"Don't come any closer!" she screamed.

He inched nearer to her in spite of her warning. "Help me, please," he said. "It's taking every ounce of strength I have, but I'm fighting off whatever this thing is inside me."

"Stay where you are." Cassie raised her hand and searched her mind for a spell.

"I don't want to hurt you," Nick said. He dropped down to his knees. "You have to believe me. Ask me anything, I swear it's really me."

Cassie knew questions would do no good, but she remembered Timothy's warning and the feeling of Adam's racing heart against her chest. *Hearts can't lie*, she told herself.

"Put your hands on your head, where I can see them," Cassie said. "And leave them there."

Nick did as he was told, and Cassie took a careful step closer.

"Stay very still," Cassie commanded, as she slowly lifted the palm of her hand to his chest.

It was a drum gone haywire. Fast as Adam's, Nick's heart was pounding as if it were trying to escape his body.

Cassie was about to pull her hand away and take off running when she noticed Nick's shoulders gently settle. He'd closed his eyes, reveling in her touch. Her contact seemed to soothe him. His breathing slowed, and then his heartbeat did, too.

He didn't move. Cassie kept her hand in place and felt his heartbeat return to a measured and regular rhythm.

"It's easier when you're near me," Nick said.

Timothy had told Cassie that love was the most powerful spell of all—that's what had made her trek out here to the caves in the first place. Her plan was to seek out Adam. But this, *this* she hadn't planned for.

Cassie released her hand from Nick's chest. "You can relax," she said.

He was sickly and sweating, barely fighting off the demon within him. But he was doing it. He was winning.

Cassie reached out again, this time to brush her fingers through his damp hair. Her love might not have been strong enough to save Adam, but Nick's love for her was proving to be strong enough to save himself. He'd managed what no one else in her Circle could do. He'd broken through the possession.

Why wasn't Adam's love strong enough to do that?

"You're going to be okay," Cassie said.

Nick's eyes filled with tears. He reached for Cassie and held her with all the energy he had left. She buried her face in his shoulder, like she used to do with Adam, and she realized just how much she needed to feel the warmth of another human body. She clung to it—to him. Nick was shaking, and she could feel herself shaking right there with him.

CHAPTER 6

Cassie lay awake, staring at her bare bedroom ceiling. By now Nick was, she hoped, sleeping downstairs in the secret room. So far, he'd been able to keep the demon at bay, but he'd told her on the boat ride back to her house that he could still sense it inside him. He'd said it with such a calm honesty, so open and unguarded, as they rowed through pitch-black night, that Cassie wasn't as frightened by the admission as she maybe should have been.

But now, in the quiet of her bedroom, Cassie worried that Nick could be a ticking time bomb. There were no guarantees the demon wouldn't get the best of him. How long could he possibly fight it off without being over-powered?

Cassie sat up, resigned, and turned on her lamp next to her bed. She couldn't sleep; her body insisted that she remain awake and ready for anything, at least tonight.

On her nightstand was the chalcedony rose Adam had given her the first day they met. She took it into her hand and admired its tiny black spirals. She turned it over to watch its gray and blue swirls sparkle beneath the lamplight, and then pressed it into her palm. The jolt of electricity that ran through her hand and up her arm was exactly how it felt to touch Adam back at the cave. The sensation was so real and true—if only she could say the same of Adam himself.

Cassie returned the chalcedony rose back to her night-stand and turned over on her side. As if the cord between Adam and Scarlett weren't enough. As if his not being able to break through the possession weren't enough. He and Scarlett had gotten together?

Cassie swallowed down the urge to cry. She would obviously have to be the one to bring Adam back, since he couldn't do it himself. And there was no time to lose.

She retrieved her father's Book of Shadows from its

hiding place beneath her bed and sprawled out with it on her bedspread, alongside a notebook. Finding the exorcism spell was the only way to put a stop to all this pain—and at the moment the pain was almost unbearable.

Cassie's eyes moved swiftly across the book's pages, searching for the section Absolom might have contributed. Every few minutes, though, she found herself zoning out, thinking back to her meeting with Timothy. He had said the exorcism spell was dangerous, that Absolom may have tampered with it.

Dangerous how? she wondered. But if it was successful, well . . . Cassie was driven by the possibility of it. She could do this, she thought. She *would* do it—but suddenly a gust of wind shot her sheer curtains open and sent her papers whirling into the air.

Cassie fell backward, momentarily disoriented. Before she could figure out what was happening, Faye was standing in her bedroom, her pitch-black hair blowing wild. It was unclear to Cassie if Faye had come through the window or if she had just appeared.

Faye's eyes were lit black coals, and she splayed her fingernails like claws. Her dark dress flapped across her body in silk waves.

All she did was casually wave her fingers, and Cassie

lost her sense of space. Her bedroom seemed to buckle beneath the overbearing energy of Faye's presence.

Cassie's vision went hazy, and the walls began to spin as if she were on a carnival ride. She couldn't tell if Faye was growing larger before her eyes, or if she herself was shrinking, or if the whole thing was a hallucination. This was nothing like the magic Cassie was used to seeing. Faye was using dark power that didn't follow any rules of nature. She didn't even need to call out spells. All she did was focus her mind and her black eyes on her intentions, and they manifested.

Cassie concentrated as best she could and called out a spell: "*I protegat ipse a veneficia!*"

Faye paused to smirk at Cassie's feeble attempt before casting another spell that drove Cassie to the ground. Then she honed in on Black John's Book of Shadows. A simple nod of her head, and the book began to tremble. It levitated up from the bed at Cassie's side, seemingly light as a feather.

That's what she came for, Cassie realized. *The book.* Cassie lunged for it, catching it in midair, and hugged it close to her chest with both arms.

Faye narrowed her searing eyes and reharnessed her energy. She appeared huge to Cassie now, hovering above her, a force of evil so sinister she couldn't be contained.

Cassie cried out.

To her own ears, Cassie's scream sounded as faint as the squeak of a mouse, a whimper lost in the wind. But somehow the book had heard her. She felt it warm to her chest like a living being. It clung to her, desperate as a child.

Faye shook with aggravation, but she would not relent. She exhaled deeply, sending a draft through the room, and then inhaled again. A dark shadow emitted from her eyes, encircling the book. She raised her outstretched hands, finally resorting to calling out a spell. *"Obedire me!"*

Her voice crashed like thunder, unnerving Cassie. The whole room shuddered, and Cassie's hair blew back from her face, but the book remained still.

The book was bound to Cassie. It was *hers*, and it might have been the only thing in this world Faye couldn't command at will.

Faye's recognition of this drove her into an even more violent rage. She roared at the room, a human hurricane, sending lamps smashing against the wall and Cassie's nightstand tumbling onto its side. The walls shook, and everything not nailed down toppled over helplessly against the force of Faye's wrath.

Cassie shouted out a protective spell to keep from being crushed, but Faye's magic was too powerful.

There was a flash of lightning and a cold wind, and then water—icy pellets of rain falling from . . . where? The ceiling? It poured down fast and hard in soaking gray sheets.

Within seconds, Cassie was up to her ankles in water, then up to her knees. She looked down and could see the clouded tops of her feet, tinted green and submerged.

But she still held tight to the book. The slithering things rose up from Faye's skin, on her face and neck, up her hands to her elbows. They squirmed like flesh-hungry maggots.

The water continued to rise over the tops of Cassie's shivering thighs. No longer able to support herself, she began to slide through it—swept in by a current. The lighter furniture in her bedroom floated and spun along with her, like driftwood in an angry river.

Finally, Cassie's head went under. She struggled, kicking her limbs and fighting to breathe, gasping at the surface, until she remembered to relax—as she would have done in the ocean if caught in a riptide. She buoyed herself up with the book, letting the water flow freely around her, and soon she was able to right herself and begin to float.

The book fed her a line: *non magis pulvia, non magis aqua.*

She said the words quietly, but they were enough.

The rain stopped falling. Cassie repeated the words again, and the raging water, which had threatened her life a moment before, began to sink down, as if a stopper had been pulled on its drain.

Cassie held tight to the book as the deluge disappeared, and it whispered something else to her: *reformidant et regredi.*

Somehow Cassie knew to aim this spell directly at Faye. She screamed it out as loud as she could.

"Reformidant et regredi!"

Faye shrieked with what sounded to Cassie like sincere pain as she shrank back down to size. She no longer radiated that blinding iridescence onto the room.

Cassie repeated the spell again, and Faye began to retreat. The storm water she'd conjured had become nothing but a damp memory, and her power was clearly depleted. It was only then that Cassie became aware of someone pounding on her bedroom door. Nick was frantically turning the handle and jiggling the lock, yelling for Cassie, asking if she was okay.

Faye glanced at the door and back at Cassie. Then just

as quickly as she had appeared, she was gone. If not for the damage left in her wake, Cassie would have believed she'd imagined the whole encounter.

A moment later Nick broke through the door.

"I'm okay," Cassie said.

Nick was wound up, breathing heavily. "Who was it?" he asked.

"Faye," Cassie said, and then corrected herself. "Beatrix."

Nick looked around Cassie's soaked and trashed bedroom, then down at the book she was still hugging close to her chest.

"You need to find a better place to hide that thing," he said. "And it wouldn't hurt for us to try to put a protective spell on the house."

Cassie stepped over a broken lamp and placed her hand on Nick's heart. She waited until she felt it slow to a regular rhythm. "You came to my rescue," she said. "Again."

Nick blushed and moved toward Cassie's bed. "Come sit with me a minute."

He closed his eyes to center his energy, and called out a simple spell. "Power of Air, make dry this room. Water damage be undone."

The wooden surfaces of Cassie's furniture lightened in color as they dried. Her bedspread crinkled like it had just come back from the laundry.

Pleased with his success, Nick plopped down and waited for Cassie to join him, but she couldn't relax just yet. She began putting her bedroom back together as quietly as she could. She righted the nightstands and gathered her papers from every corner of the floor.

"Faye couldn't command the book," Cassie said, as she cleaned. "But with all that power she could have easily killed me to get it. She could have destroyed the entire house and everyone inside it with barely the blink of an eye."

"But she didn't," Nick said. "So the book was obviously not all she was after."

"She must want me alive for some reason," Cassie said. "Maybe the ancestors even *need* me alive."

She joined Nick on the bed, finally. "Do you think that's just my own wishful thinking? That they don't want me dead?"

Nick wrapped his strong arms around her. "I think you're special, Cassie, and they know that."

"But they may come after you," Cassie said. "Or my mom. Luckily she took a pill to help her sleep tonight.

Can you imagine her reaction if she'd been the one to break through my door instead of you? The shock alone may have killed her."

She thought for another minute. "They'll probably go after Max, too. He's the last hunter left in New Salem."

"Max is pretty tough," Nick said. "He can take care of himself. But if you're worried about it, you should warn him. Go talk to him tomorrow. I can keep a close watch on your mom and begin researching a protective spell."

Nick's presence quieted Cassie's aching loneliness. His friendship meant the world to her at the moment. "I don't want you to go back downstairs," she said.

Nick pointed to the plush chair in the corner of the room. "Why don't I sleep right there tonight?" he asked. "The closer we are, the better it is for both of us."

"But you'll be so uncomfortable," Cassie said.

Nick grabbed a pillow and the extra blanket off the edge of Cassie's bed. "I'll be just fine."

Cassie could feel her eyes closing. "If you're sure," she said, already drifting off. At last she would be able to get some sleep.

CHAPTER 7

Cassie walked down Crowhaven Road the next morning alert to her surroundings, ready for anything. If the ancestors were following her and sensed the book hidden deep in her bag—if they jumped her, mauled her—she was prepared to fight.

She knocked gently on the red wooden door she hadn't thought she'd ever come within ten feet of. Her knuckles on the door's surface made a dense muffled sound, not hollow like she'd thought it would. It was solid oak.

She looked around apprehensively and waited.

Max opened the door a few inches and poked his head outside. Then he instantly began to shut it in Cassie's face. She had expected this reaction, so she was ready with a spell to hold the door open.

"*Aperire non clausa,*" she said softly but firmly.

No matter how hard Max tried, he couldn't force the door closed. He looked furious.

"I came here to warn you," Cassie said. "You might be in serious danger."

"I have nothing left to lose," Max said.

Cassie peeked inside the door and saw an older man and woman in the kitchen.

"Who are they?" Cassie asked.

"Family friends," Max said. "My new guardians, now that I'm parentless."

"They could be in danger, too," Cassie said. "Please, Max. Just hear me out, and then I'll leave you alone. I promise."

Maybe it was the regret in her eyes or the desperation of her voice. It was impossible to know for sure what convinced him, but Max stepped aside and allowed Cassie to enter.

Once inside, she closed the door behind them.

The house itself was modest but clean, less extravagant than Cassie had imagined. It was the house of a family that moved around a lot, filled with mismatched furniture, most likely from a thrift store or the cheap local shops. Some things were still in brown boxes stacked in the corner of the living room, and hardly anything was hung on the flat beige walls. The house was all function, no decoration.

Cassie followed Max up a narrow carpeted stairway to his bedroom. The moment he opened its door, Cassie sensed how much it differed from the rest of the monotone house.

Max had painted the space a soothing light blue, and he'd taken great care to adorn the walls with pictures. One wall was a grid of shelves crowded with shiny sports trophies and awards. It was neat and clean, not a speck of dust anywhere.

Cassie could tell Max had gone out of his way to make his bedroom comfortable—to make it feel like his own, like home.

On a long rectangular dresser were a variety of photographs set in frames. Cassie ambled toward them. The largest one was of Max's parents, each holding one of his hands when he was just a toddler. They appeared to be at a park. Surrounding that photo were portraits of him and various friends at different ages, and landscapes of other places he'd lived. Other countries. Max had once petted a baby Bengal tiger. He'd jumped from the top of a cascading waterfall. He'd climbed mountains. Cassie picked up the most majestic of the mountain photos, the one of Max red-faced and bundled in gear at the peak of a snowy summit.

"That's the top of Mount Kilimanjaro," he said. "It's the highest mountain in Africa."

Cassie set the frame back in place and looked at Max in a new way. "What a life you've lived," she said.

There was so much more going on beneath the surface of Max than she'd ever imagined. No wonder Diana fell so hopelessly in love with him.

"May I sit down?" she asked.

Max nodded but remained standing. Cassie explained, to the best of her abilities, what had really happened that night in the caves. She described how Scarlett had deceived the Circle, and she told Max that anything for which he blamed Diana wasn't her fault. Finally, Cassie broke the news about how Diana and the rest of the Circle were now possessed.

"The spirit that has control over Diana might try to use Diana's love for you as a sort of weapon," she said. "That's what I came here to warn you about."

Max finally allowed himself to sit down across from Cassie. He took a deep breath. "I really don't want anything to do with this," he said. "I'd rather forget this whole thing ever happened."

"I get that, believe me," Cassie said. "I'm so sorry you got dragged into all this."

Max's eyes filled with a sadness Cassie couldn't identify. It wasn't for his father, or even for Diana. It was older than that: a long-standing sadness he held inside, tinged with a sense of responsibility.

"What are the spirits after?" he asked.

"I'm not entirely sure. Revenge would be my guess. Most of them were killed by Outsiders for being witches. And I know they want my father's Book of Shadows."

Cassie had been carrying the book with her, thinking it was safer with her than at home, unprotected. She pulled it out of her bag.

Max eyed the book apprehensively. "What do they need it for?"

Cassie considered what could occur if the spirits did get hold of the book. "I honestly have no idea what they'd be capable of," she said. "What I do know is that all dark magic can be traced back to the early days of this book. And to these ancestor spirits."

"Dark magic," Max repeated.

Cassie nodded. "The magic your family line devoted their lives to stopping."

Warily, Max took the book from Cassie's hands and examined it. "If you need to keep this book hidden from the spirits, you should leave it here." He paused. "If you think it'll keep New Salem any safer, I mean."

"Max, they're going to come after you," Cassie said. "That's what I'm trying to tell you. They'll want to destroy any threats, and you're the last hunter left in town."

"But they're not coming after me for the book," Max said. A half-grin snuck across his face. "They wouldn't expect you to give it to a witch-hunter for safekeeping."

Cassie realized he was right. The ancestors would never think to search for the book at Max's house. She also realized that his sense of duty, the oath he took as a hunter to protect non-witches from dark magic, now made him her ally—in spite of everything.

"That's a brave offer," Cassie said. She tried to convey with her eyes her appreciation and her trust in him. A witch and a hunter joining forces was no small feat. "The only problem is that I need to continue studying the book, to find a spell that will save my friends. If I don't figure out a way to get the demons out of their bodies by the next full moon, their souls will be lost forever."

Max's slight smile disappeared as quickly as it had come. Cassie could tell his heart ached at the thought of Diana being lost this way.

"You need to perform an exorcism," he said. "I can help you with that."

A glimpse of sunlight seemed to fill the room. Of course. As a hunter, Max might know more about fighting evil spirits than Cassie ever could.

"Thank you," Cassie said. "Diana would be—"

"Don't thank me," Max said abruptly. "And don't even say her name to me. I'm doing this for the safety of this town and the innocent people in it. Not for you or Diana."

Cassie was taken aback, but she understood. Max had every right to still be angry. She nodded, knowing not to thank him aloud again.

"I'll take a look through this"—Max tossed the book onto his desk—"and let you know what I find."

Cassie recognized that was her cue to leave. "Okay" was all she said before letting herself out of his room.

She quietly stepped down the carpeted stairs. The man and woman were still in the kitchen, seated at a table, eating breakfast. They didn't acknowledge her as she slipped out of the door. How would they react if they knew the man whose house they were in had died at her hands? Accident or not, Cassie had to live with that fact for the rest of her life. And so did Max.

CHAPTER 8

Nick caught Cassie watching him and smiled. He stuck out his tongue and crossed his eyes like a clown.

"Sorry," Cassie said. "I don't mean to stare."

"That's okay. I don't blame you. But you can trust me to tell you if I sense something strange coming on." He laughed and put his arm around her. "Besides, the more I'm with you, the better I feel."

Cassie and Nick were walking along Crowhaven Road. Nick pulled a handful of glossy green leaves from a low-hanging sumac tree. He tore off little divots as they walked, leaving a trail of misshapen pieces behind them. So far Nick had remained strong enough to persevere through the possession.

Since Cassie had led Nick out of the cave, there were moments she could sense his exhaustion, and it pained her to see how hard he was working. Then other times were like this. Easy, comfortable, cozy. They were able to enjoy a pleasant breeze and the warm morning sun on their backs.

It gave Cassie hope that things with her other friends could still turn out okay. If Nick could be saved, they could all be saved.

The wind stirred, and Nick's face took on a softness in the sunlight that Cassie hadn't seen in a long while. She was so moved by it that, without thinking, she reached out her hand to stroke his cheek.

He leaned in to her fingers.

They were both so caught up in the moment that they didn't notice Scarlett and Adam step out onto the sidewalk in front of them, blocking their path forward.

"I hope I'm not interrupting anything." Scarlett crossed her arms over her chest. "Got a minute to talk?"

"No, we don't," Nick said.

Scarlett was unfazed. She appeared healthy, which meant she had regained all her strength. Adam kept close to her side, protective, domineering. Cassie couldn't bear to look at him.

"I don't have the book on me," she said. "Now if you'll excuse us, we're going to be late for school."

"Forget school." Scarlett guffawed. "I've got a much more enticing offer."

"We're not interested." Cassie made an attempt to storm past them, pulling Nick along with her, but Scarlett blocked their way again.

"Just hear us out," Scarlett said. She twirled a ringlet of her red hair around her pointer finger. "Otherwise I'm going to have to get vicious, and we both know how that usually ends."

Cassie scoped out the surrounding area. There weren't any other people on the street, only a few stray pigeons clucking on an overhead wire. If Scarlett and Adam wanted to, they could use magic against Cassie and Nick without much consequence.

Cassie noticed Nick's teeth were clenched, and his chest heaved up and down with each labored breath.

Adam watched him. For any sign of the demon getting the best of him, Cassie assumed. He seemed to be calling to it, summoning it.

"What do you want?" Cassie said, terrified Adam just might push Nick over the edge. "We don't have all day."

"You're almost there," Adam whispered to Nick. "I can

feel how close you are to crossing over. Can't you?"

"Leave Nick out of this!" Cassie shouted.

Adam looked at her, amused. But Scarlett remained serious. "Come with us to the abandoned warehouse on State Street," she said. "Where the Circle is staying."

"Why?" Cassie asked.

Scarlett smiled wide. "Isn't it obvious? We want you, Cassie. To be part of our Circle."

"You want the book," Cassie said. "Faye made that pretty clear when she trashed my bedroom last night and tried to steal it. What's in there that you want so badly?"

"Everything," Adam said, his face blank.

"But it's *you* who means something to us," Scarlett added, in a more innocent tone of voice. "Both of you. The book would just be a bonus."

"Don't insult my intelligence," Cassie said.

"It's true, sis. And you know it's the truth, because we all benefit from having a complete Circle. You can appreciate that as well as anyone."

"Your Circle isn't ours," Nick shouted, loud enough to make Cassie jump.

Cassie looked at Nick and saw the obvious strain on his face. He was losing his cool, struggling to maintain his defenses against the demon. Sweat poured down from his forehead, and his hands shook. Cassie worried she might be losing him.

Adam eyed Nick with satisfaction. "What's the matter, Nicholas? Aren't you feeling well?"

Cassie placed her hand on Nick's back to calm him. "He's fine," she said. "And he's right. Your Circle isn't ours, and it never will be."

Scarlett let out a sigh. "Never say never, Cassie."

"Never," Cassie said, louder. As she spoke, she could feel Nick trembling. She could make out the rapid thumping of his heart. She rubbed small ovals on his T-shirt, silently willing the demon inside him away. But his heart raced faster and faster.

"That's a good boy," Adam said.

The irises of Nick's eyes darkened, and Cassie noticed a wiggling on his neck, what looked like a vein worming its way onto his face.

"Mark my words," Scarlett said to Cassie. "You'll change your mind. It's only a matter of time."

Cassie held tight to Nick as he calmed himself back to normal.

Scarlett grabbed Adam's hand and pulled him toward her. "He's stronger than he looks, isn't he?" she said to Adam. "He's got it for her that bad."

Adam narrowed his eyes and snaked his arm around Scarlett's waist. "It won't last forever," he said. "Nothing does." Together they crossed the street, close as lovers, Scarlett's red hair bouncing along behind her like an accomplice.

"You should have accepted my friendly invitation while you had the chance, Cassie," Scarlett called back over her shoulder.

Cassie didn't have the time to deal with Scarlett's threat or her manipulative mind games. She turned to Nick and searched his face and body for more signs of trouble.

Adam's last comment had rattled him. His eyes were black pinpoints, and the skin on his face squirmed.

"Nick," Cassie said, rubbing his back. "Stay with me."

He groaned quietly and subconsciously at Cassie's touch.

"You're Nick Armstrong," Cassie said. "Your parents' names were Nicholas and Sharon."

Nick's face softened in a way that made Cassie believe she was reaching the real him in there.

"Your favorite song is 'Beast of Burden' by the Rolling Stones," she said.

"I remember," Nick said without looking at her. "Do

you remember our first kiss? I'd just been listening to that song."

Cassie continued rubbing his back with one hand. With the other she monitored the beating of his heart.

"It was the night you and the girls did that candle ceremony," Nick said. "And you'd gone out alone to bury that trust box, and Black John attacked you."

He appeared to get lost in the recollection. "You were so scared, but you still looked so beautiful in the moonlight. And your lips were so soft . . ."

Cassie felt the rhythm of Nick's heart slow beneath her hand.

"How about one of the most vivid memories of my life?" Nick asked. "The time we were on the bluff and the hunters attacked us with fire. A lightning bolt struck that tree, and—"

"And you jumped in front of it and saved my life," Cassie said. How could she forget?

"And when we were at the spring dance," Nick said. "It was just the two of us when Scarlett showed up."

Cassie finished Nick's sentence for him. "And you risked your life by performing magic out in the open, getting marked to save me."

Nick nodded and smiled.

It occurred to Cassie that Nick was recalling these memories to hold on to who he really was, but they were actually proof of his persistent love for her since she'd known him. His *love*.

"I'm okay now," Nick said. "I'm still with you."

His heartbeat was steady and regular, almost peaceful. Cassie removed her hand from his chest.

Nick was so obviously beaten down and in pain, Cassie had the urge to cry. But she couldn't lose her nerve and let him see her weaken now.

"You did well," she said. "You managed to bring yourself back."

She put her arm around him, and they continued their walk to school. "You're the strongest boy I know," she said.

CHAPTER 9

Cassie arrived at her locker to find it wide open and emptied. Ransacked was more like it. All her books were strewn about the floor, split at their spines. She'd been at school less than an hour, and the possessed Circle had already begun wreaking havoc.

She looked to the left and right, then began picking up her books. The hallway was crowded with students, but hardly anyone paid her much attention. It wasn't until she piled the last textbook into her locker that Deborah, Sean, and Doug came thundering down the hall.

They walked shoulder to shoulder. They were dressed in all black. Cassie could see the sheen in their eyes.

They were performing magic right out in the open.

Like Faye, they were capable of doing magic without having to call out spells. With only the power of their minds, they took aim at people in the hallway. Sean focused on Mr. Tanner, a teacher Cassie knew had once unfairly punished him. Mr. Tanner's briefcase flew from his hand, cracking open onto the hallway floor. Its contents—test papers and attendance sheets, late passes and pencils—swirled up around him in a tornado.

There was no longer any doubt in Cassie's mind that the spirits were somehow absorbing the feelings of her friends and using them for their own purposes. The possession was becoming more seamless and, most likely, closer to permanent.

Mr. Tanner's face and neck reddened as he tried to catch hold of his things. He was trembling, looking around embarrassed and terrified, unable to fathom where this stiff wind came from.

Sean stepped in front of him, meeting his eyes. He smiled wickedly, then snapped his fingers. Mr. Tanner's belongings dropped to the floor.

Deborah shot Cassie a menacing look that made her understand the danger unfolding at school this morning was only the beginning. Cassie wanted to turn away but found she couldn't. Deborah was forcing her to watch what would happen next, as if she'd peeled Cassie's eyelids back and fastened them open with clothespins.

Sally Waltman was unlucky enough to turn the corner at that moment. The bullying smile on Deborah's face twisted into something more frightening. She glanced upward, and Cassie followed her line of vision, knowing she had only a few seconds to react.

Cassie leapt before she fully knew why and knocked Sally out of the way just before a fluorescent light fell from the ceiling. It shattered on the floor where Sally had been just a moment before.

Everyone nearby dove for cover. Shards of glass slashed through the air. A single sliver nicked Cassie's cheek.

Mr. Humphries came running down the hall, commanding everyone out of the way. Cassie stood up from where she was lying on the floor, but Sally remained stretched out, facedown.

Deborah winked at Cassie and then gave Sean and Doug a nudge. They moved along, out of the way, blending with the other students. Cassie didn't have it in her to chase after them.

Mr. Humphries turned Sally over, ordering the cluster of onlookers to stand back. Her eyes were closed, and

Cassie couldn't tell if she was breathing. Specks of shiny glass dotted her pink cardigan.

Mr. Humphries squeezed Sally's wrist and felt her neck for a pulse as the surrounding crowd of students gathered closer and closer to her unmoving body.

"Somebody call an ambulance!" Mr. Humphries screamed out, but in the next second Sally's eyes opened and sharpened with a gradual consciousness to the situation. She tried to sit up.

Cassie exhaled, realizing only then that she'd been holding her breath. She and Sally locked eyes before Sally checked her body over for injuries.

"I'm okay," she said to Mr. Humphries.

Cassie could see that only her hands were speckled with tiny dots of blood. The rest of her body had been spared, thankfully.

Mr. Humphries's face was white as a sheet. "Cassie, will you take her to the nurse?" he asked. "I have to find the head custodian. That light was obviously not installed properly. She could have been killed!"

Sally was visibly okay—just shaken—but Mr. Humphries might have been even more upset than she was. Cassie agreed to take Sally to the nurse to appease him.

Once he was gone and out of earshot, Cassie put her arm around Sally. "You're safe now," she said.

The crowd dispersed, and Sally looked at Cassie warily. "Do you think that falling light was really the custodian's fault?"

Cassie shook her head. Of all the Outsiders at school, Sally was the only one who knew the truth about the Circle and their magic—and she'd proven herself an ally. She didn't deserve to be placated or lied to.

"No," Cassie said. "That was no accident."

Sally was still trembling.

"But I'm working on it," Cassie added.

"Let's just go to the assembly," Sally said. "I'm fine."

The auditorium was full by the time Cassie and Sally arrived, but none of her possessed friends were to be seen. Cassie tried to breathe easy. She hoped they'd taunted her enough for one day and had gone back to the warehouse.

Sally spotted Nick in the crowd, and they joined him.

"Why do you have glass in your hair?" Nick asked, as he pulled a tiny sparkling shard from Sally's rust-colored curls. It resembled a diamond earring.

"It's a long story," Cassie said. "I'll tell you later."

Mr. Lanning appeared on stage and tapped on the

microphone. Once he quieted everyone down he began to say a few words about Principal Boylan.

"We're gathered here to mourn the death of a kind and generous man," he said. "A man we unfortunately didn't have the pleasure of knowing longer."

He paused to let his words settle over the crowd in waves. "By now you've all heard about the terrible car accident that took Principal Boylan's life. And I'm sure you're all still processing the pain and confusion that comes with this tragedy. For this reason, there will be grief counselors on hand immediately following this assembly. But first, it's with a heavy heart that I'd like to call Principal Boylan's son, Max, to the stage."

Nobody seemed sure if they should clap as Max took his place at the podium. There were a few stray coughs. All eyes scrutinized his every movement.

How awful, Cassie thought as she watched Max adjust the microphone and swallow down the lump in his throat, *for him to be obligated to say a few words about his father's "accident."* But Max carried himself with the utmost dignity as he spoke. His voice echoed over the auditorium.

"My father was a leader," Max said. "A man with a strong moral code, who never abandoned what he believed to be right."

Cassie recognized many of those same traits in Max, too. Watching him and listening to him, and thinking back to all the photographs in his room, Cassie truly understood his goodness.

"He cared about this school and this town very much," Max continued. "He wanted what was best for all of us, and he worked for that every day of his life."

Max appeared to be wrapping up, finally reaching the end of those treacherous minutes in the spotlight, when both doors to the auditorium swung open, crashing loudly against the wall.

All heads turned to witness the disturbance. Every muscle in Cassie's body tightened.

It was the possessed Circle. Five at one door, five at the other. They formed a line barricading the exit.

Diana's posture was foreboding. Faye's dark hair tumbled onto her shoulders like a black shadow. Adam's eyes were electric with vengeance.

Just then the only empty seat in the auditorium, the one in the front row where Max had been sitting, burst into flames.

Mr. Lanning rushed for the fire extinguisher but was thrown backward—through the air and hard onto the ground—when it also exploded into flames. The fire spread quickly: up the wall, across the timbered auditorium floor, flaring like kindling.

Teachers and students shoved one another, trying to escape through the narrow exit doors. The room became a jumble of screams and elbows; the weak and small were trampled beneath the bigger shoes of the strong. Cassie lost sight of the ancestors in the smoke and panic.

She turned to Sally. "Get out of here. Nick and I will do what we can."

More seats exploded, and fire swelled high into the aisles. Sally crouched down below the heavy cloud of smoke and crawled on her belly to safety.

Nick raised his arms and called out: "No air for fire! No air for fire, no air for fire!"

The flames momentarily became still, and then bowed to him, shrinking gradually—suffocating.

Max was standing motionless on stage with his arms down at his sides. He looked directly at Cassie with his mouth hanging half open.

Nick continued to talk down the flames, overpowering the fire with his will. Through the lessening black smoke, Cassie took inventory of the bodies rolling and coughing, or lying unconscious on the ground. She ran toward Max but was distracted by a low rumble, then a loud crack.

She stopped short.

The ceiling overhead began falling down in pieces all around her—slowly at first, then in a rapid avalanche of cracked plaster and splintered wooden beams.

Cassie covered her head with her hands and turned around just in time to see Nick knocked down by the falling debris. Max had also been buried, out of sight. No one made a sound.

Cassie looked up, thinking she might actually see blue sky, so much of the ceiling had come down. And there they were: Adam, Diana, Faye, and the rest of her friends, hovering in the air. They were levitating, safely among the only standing rafters left to the auditorium's roof.

Cassie closed her eyes and searched her mind for a spell. She steadied her breath and called to the dark pit that resided in her belly.

She felt herself flush with heat from the inside out, and that ominous feeling from deep within rose up. She knew that it was her dark magic—the only magic that would be strong enough to overpower the ancestors. Cassie gave herself over to it, allowing the spell to come to her: *Cadens obruta, consurget.*

Like vomit, the words spewed from her mouth. "*Cadens obruta, consurget!*"

As Cassie raised her arms, the fallen wreckage rose with them.

"*Consurget!*" she shouted.

All the wood and beams and broken shards of plaster that had rained down over Cassie's head flew back up from the floor toward the ceiling.

Her friends ducked and dodged the oncoming wave of debris. Shafts of plywood and metal shot up at them like arrows.

"*Duratus!*" Cassie called out, and they were unable to move. They were swiftly becoming buried from the ground up, pinned to the ceiling with more and more rubble.

No longer trapped beneath the wreckage, Nick climbed to his feet. He wiped the shadow of plaster and ash from his eyes.

"Check on Max," Cassie said.

But Max, too, had climbed back up to a standing position. His face was battered and his lip leaked blood, but aside from that he appeared unharmed. He brushed the white dust and dirt from his clothes.

Nick touched a swelling bruise above his eyebrow. "How long do you think they'll be trapped up there?" he asked.

Somewhere in the distance, outside the school building, Cassie could hear a siren coming closer. "Long enough for us to get out of here." She turned to Max. "What do you say we get right to work on that exorcism spell?"

"I'd say we're overdue," Max said, making his way through the ruined auditorium toward the exit.

CHAPTER 10

Max leaned both his skinned elbows on the tabletop as he hovered over the page of Black John's Book of Shadows they were trying to translate. He and Nick were banged up from the auditorium, with fat lips and puffy bruises purpling their faces, but neither of them showed any pain—tough guys that they were.

Max pointed at an odd triangular shape. "This symbol is a triskelion within a circle," he said. "I recognize it from somewhere."

Cassie and Nick had gone directly to Max's house from the auditorium so they could study the book together.

They were shut up in his room with the door locked and Black John's book open between them.

Cassie took her eyes away from the symbol momentarily to watch Max pull a few cardboard boxes out from beneath his bed. There were many boxes under there, Cassie noticed. The ones visible appeared to be filled with old maps and yellowed papers, coins and amulets. One was stacked full with leather journals. That was the box Max dug through.

He pulled out an ancient-looking book.

"Is that your own Book of Shadows?" Nick asked.

"Pretty much. Well, the hunter version of it anyway," Max said. "Same idea."

The book was delicately bound, and when he opened it, dust fell from its spine. By the writing and markings covering its pages, Cassie could tell it had been passed down for generations.

In a few minutes, Max found the page he was looking for. "Here," he said.

Nick took the book from Max's hands. "I don't believe it. It's the same triangle shape." He placed the two books side by side.

The symbols were identical.

"My ancestors tried exorcism as a way to fight off witches," Max said. "That's what this page in my book talks about."

The text Max pointed to was partially written in what Cassie recognized as Latin. The rest was composed of an ancient language she couldn't identify.

"It didn't work for them," Max said. "But they did know about this symbol."

"Which means this page of my father's book must contain information about performing an exorcism," Cassie said, finally catching up to Max's train of thought. "Otherwise why else would the symbol be printed on it?"

"Exactly. It'll still take some time to translate," Max said. "But it's good to know we're on the right track. This section of your father's book is definitely the area we should be focusing on. The entire exorcism spell might be right here on this page."

Cassie's pulse raced. She felt as though she'd been shaken awake. "You're the best," she said to Max. "You know that?"

Max looked away, not meeting her eyes. "I'm only doing what I can to make sure more people don't get hurt."

"That's as good a reason as any," Nick said, seeming to appreciate Max in a whole new way. He gave him a brotherly smack on the back.

Cassie copied the page with the symbol on it from her father's book onto a fresh sheet of paper. Max would still hold on to the book for safekeeping, but now Cassie had a copy of what she needed to continue working on.

The papers crinkled as she stuffed them deep into her bag. "This was the best thing to happen to me all day," she said.

Max squinted at her and allowed himself a half-smile. "On a day like today, that's really not saying much."

"Good point," Cassie said, and laughed.

<hr />

Enjoying a sense of accomplishment, Cassie and Nick stepped in the front door to Cassie's house. They each carried a brown bag from the grocery store filled with ice cream and potato chips and assorted other goodies to fuel their night's work translating the spell. Then Cassie heard a crunching beneath her shoes.

"Shattered glass," Nick said. "Could only mean one thing."

They both dropped their bags on the floor and then noticed the path of overturned chairs leading to Cassie's mother. She was tied to the one chair upright in the kitchen, gagged and unable to speak.

"Untie her," Cassie said. "I'll check upstairs."

Cassie heard Diana, Adam, and Faye ripping apart her bedroom before she saw them. Everything they touched, they left tattered and torn.

"You're wasting your time," Cassie said from the doorway. "The book isn't here."

Diana was the first to look up. "Tell us where it is, or we'll burn this whole house down."

"We're good at burning things," Faye said. "As you know."

"And I'm good at putting fires out," Cassie said. "As *you* know."

Adam narrowed his eyes. "She's becoming less fearful," he said. "Let's show her why that's a mistake."

Together, Adam and Faye stared Cassie down. She fell to her knees, gasping for air—but she had anticipated this attack. This time she was ready.

When she'd tapped into her dark magic earlier in the day, it had left a resonance. A tingle of that power remained on the tip of her tongue and fingers. She urged it to come again, more easily this time. The words uttered themselves: *Audire sonum malum.*

Suddenly Adam, Faye, and Diana all covered their ears with their hands. They wailed. Whatever spell had come to Cassie hit the spirits like a screeching alarm.

Cassie felt her strength flare. She stood up tall and repeated the spell again.

Her friends backed away, crouched over, trying to escape the sound blaring inside their own heads. They could barely drag themselves to the doorway.

Cassie stepped aside, allowing them to stumble by her and down the stairs. She followed them, guiding them with her spell, past Nick and her mother in the kitchen and out the way they came in.

Cassie pursued them until the blur of their doubled-over bodies disappeared down the block, lost to the sunshine. Then she rushed to her mother, who was untied but sitting in the same chair, drinking a glass of water.

"I'm fine," she said. "I only wish I could have stopped them."

Nick surveyed the damage their visitors had done to the front door and windows. "I can replace the glass and repair the door," he said. "But they'll probably just break through it again."

Cassie's mother appeared unreasonably calm considering what she'd just been through. She rubbed at the tender rope burns on her arms and wrists, but she spoke loudly and clearly. "We have to take stronger precautions."

"Nick and I have been trying to research a guarding spell to protect the house," Cassie said. "But we haven't been able to find one that would work on a demon."

"I know one," her mother said matter-of-factly. "I still remember the spell your grandmother used when she built the secret room."

She gave Cassie a somber look. "It's been a long time since we've had to worry about demon spirits entering the house."

Nick had been pushing some broken glass into a small pile near the door. When he looked up, he asked, "Does that include me? Do I count as a demon or a human?"

Cassie's mother blushed, feeling Nick's shame for him. "You'll be fine here as long as the spirit doesn't take full possession of your body."

Nick returned his focus to the pile of glass. "Then that should be no problem," he said. "As long as I've got Cassie pulling for me, there's no way that'll happen."

Cassie looked at Nick's face and saw so much weariness there, but also extraordinary strength. She wasn't sure what she would have done without him.

CHAPTER 11

Cassie and Nick were sprawled on the couch, watching a movie to unwind. They'd treated themselves to a day home from school, so she and Nick could make the necessary repairs to the house after yesterday's attack. But they'd finished the job in record time, leaving the rest of the afternoon for just the two of them. The movie was a romantic comedy, one Cassie had seen before and loved—yet she couldn't help watching Nick as much as she watched the film.

She wasn't searching him for a sign of the demon any longer. This was different, looking more for the comfort Nick's face brought her. His dark eyes and strong jaw, the way he could focus on her in such a way that made her feel like the only person in the world, or at least the only one that mattered. And he was warm. Always, like a heated rock to curl up beside.

While watching the screen, Nick subconsciously ran his fingers up the length of Cassie's arm, from her wrist to her elbow, and back down again.

Or maybe it wasn't subconsciously.

Cassie felt the sensation in her whole body. She knew she should pull her arm away, but instead she found herself closing her eyes to better enjoy it.

From the sound of the movie alone, she recognized the scene of the hero getting to kiss his dream girl for the first time. When she reopened her eyes, she found Nick watching her as he continued stroking her arm.

Finally, she pulled away from him.

Nick clicked off the TV and leaned in closer.

Cassie felt her face get hot. Was he going to kiss her? She could tell he wanted to. His breath was heavy, needy, close to her ear.

"Nick, no," Cassie said.

He exhaled with frustration and looked down. "Because of Adam?"

Cassie nodded.

"But these past few days have been . . . and you know how I feel about you, Cassie."

If only Adam were as strong as Nick, Cassie thought. Why wasn't *his* love enough to break through the possession?

"You know how I feel about you, too," Cassie said.

Nick shook his head. "Not really."

He tried to reach for Cassie's hand again, but she didn't let him. "I think we should get back to work translating the spell."

She stood up and made her way to the stairs without looking Nick in the eyes.

He followed behind her, sullenly.

Up in her room, Cassie went right to the top drawer of her desk. She opened it roughly and pushed aside the decoy pile of sketchbooks and folders set there to hide the pages she'd copied from her father's book.

Cassie unfolded the pages carefully upon her desk, straightening out their edges. To the naked eye, they appeared to be blank because of the protective spell she'd cast on them.

Nick plopped down on her bed as she rested her palms upon the papers. She whispered the secret incantation to reveal their text:

Hidden words, dark to pale
I who concealed you, now lift your veil

Gradually the familiar ink-black swirl of Cassie's handwriting reappeared.

She sat at her desk, bent over the pages, examining the strange triangular symbol that she hadn't been able to get out of her head since Max pointed it out to her. A triskelion within a circle, Max had called it. Once believed to exorcise evil spirits. Other than that symbol, the text on the page was mostly nonsense to Cassie, a jumble of ink that meant nothing.

She stared at the string of writing before her until the lines all blurred together. There were a few characters she understood, a few dozen ancient words, a handful of symbols. But it was the same characters and words that she understood every time, and the same ones she didn't understand over and over again. She wasn't figuring out anything new.

Nick lay on her bed playing a game on his phone.

"Nick," she said, trying to regain his attention. "I don't understand why translating these pages has been so difficult."

Nick tossed his phone down and joined Cassie at her desk, standing behind her, with his hands on the back of her chair. "Well, if you can't translate it, no one can," he said, sounding annoyed. "You're the one who's bound to the book. And this isn't even a language." He smacked the papers with his fingers. "Don't your translation skills come from within you? From your blood?"

"That's just it," Cassie said. "Timothy said Absolom might have doctored the exorcism, which means he probably made it a dark-magic spell. But it must be a level of darkness even I can't access. I've tried and tried, but I just can't do it."

"Then we're doomed," Nick exclaimed, sweeping the papers off Cassie's desk.

He was sweating, and his chest heaved up and down with his breath.

Could their conversation downstairs have left him upset enough to stir the demon?

He turned around so Cassie couldn't see his face.

"Nick, come closer," Cassie said. She put her hand on his back, but he shrugged it off and bent down to pick up the papers from the floor.

"I have it under control," he said, shaking the papers at her. "It's just this spell—"

He stared at the writing on the crinkled page in his grip. "It's . . ."

Suddenly his eyes turned black. His upper lip curled oddly to the left. He began to mumble: *Discedere, malum spiritus. Exi, seductor. Relinquere haec innocens corpora.*

Cassie tore the papers away from him and smacked her hand onto his heart. It was beating faster than even Adam's had, that night at the caves.

"Calm down!" she screamed. "Stay with me, Nick."

He took a few deep breaths, and his heartbeat slowed, thankfully, but his eyes were still darker than their usual mahogany brown.

"I could read it," he said, with a tremble in his voice. "For a few seconds I could understand the spell."

Cassie glanced at the indecipherable text on the paper in her hand and then back at Nick. It all became clear. "Not you," she said. "The demon inside you."

Nick wiped the sweat from his brow. "I could read it because I'm possessed?"

Cassie nodded. "Whatever Blak ancestor of mine that's trying to possess you can decipher the spell."

They both got quiet as they allowed this new possibility to settle over them: Nick would have to give himself over to the demon in order to translate the spell.

"No," Cassie said, before Nick even opened his mouth to speak. "It's too dangerous."

"It's our only hope," Nick insisted. "I have to give up control to the demon. Then I'll come back again."

"But what if you can't?"

Nick took the papers from Cassie and went to her desk. He let his eyes pass quickly over the text. "I'm strong enough," he said. "And once the spell is translated, you'll be able to rid the whole Circle of demons."

Cassie wanted to believe that Nick would be able to return, that she would be able to bring him back—but she couldn't really be sure.

"I don't want to do this," she said.

But Nick had already opened Cassie's notebook to a blank page and picked up a pen.

Cassie was terrified of what they were about to attempt, but Nick refused to be deterred. He closed his eyes for a moment, pen in hand, with the spell before him.

"I know I can do it," he said, and when he reopened his eyes, they were black as marbles.

Cassie stepped back.

Nick sat up, unusually rigid. For a few seconds, he made no sound or movement. Then he began talking in a voice that wasn't his own, in a language he could have never known—a low, guttural growl. And then he began writing.

Cassie watched from over his shoulder.

Nick's whole body trembled, his neck twisted in impossible ways, but he continued to move the pen across the paper.

His script was shaky but clearly legible. Across the top of the blank notebook page, he wrote:

Rite

For

Exorcism

He was doing it. Cassie could hardly believe her eyes.

The veins on the insides of Nick's arms wriggled beneath the skin. A disturbing high-pitched sound escaped his mouth, the screech of something sinful and starving.

The letters spurted from his pen faster and faster. He worked for about two minutes without pause. Then with one sudden motion he slammed the pen down onto the desk and looked up at Cassie. His face bubbled; his lips effervesced.

"Cassandra," he said. His voice was unfathomable, a bottomless cavern. "Get me out of here."

Cassie shuddered. *Get who out of where?* "Nick? Is that you?"

Nick's eyes rolled back into his head. His whole body shook, and he fell onto the floor, convulsing.

Cassie leaned over him, smacking his cheek, pressing on his racing heart. "Nick, come back to me," she screamed. "It's Cassie, please come back to me."

A gurgling sound came out of Nick's mouth, and she realized he was choking on his own tongue. "Nick!" she yelled, pulling him upright and hugging him close to her chest. She held him so they were heart to heart.

"Please don't leave me," she said into his ear. "I can't go on without you."

The awful gurgling sound stopped, but Nick's body still convulsed.

"I've got you," Cassie said. "I'm here, and I'm not letting you go."

She kissed his soaking-wet head and his face. She encircled his torso so tightly they could have melded together as one.

Gradually, the shaking lessened.

Cassie continued holding him, rocking him back and forth, as his heartbeat began to steady.

In those few minutes, the spell ceased to be relevant. Nick, heavy in her arms, was her whole world.

It was a while before he coughed and startled himself awake. She reawakened with him. He blinked his eyelashes rapidly and looked around the room. When he locked eyes with Cassie, she saw they were back to their normal color.

"What just happened?" Nick asked.

Cassie reached for the notebook that now contained the full text of the exorcism spell. "This happened," she said. "You did it."

"And I made it back?"

"Yes," Cassie said, throwing her arms around him again. "You did."

Nick was exhausted by the possession. Cassie had to help him to the bed and give him water to drink. She watched him sleep for almost an hour, following the rise and fall of his chest, listening to his even breaths. She wanted to touch him but wouldn't dare disturb his slumber. He'd given everything, and now he needed his rest.

While Nick continued to sleep, Cassie examined the spell. It was mystifying to look at, all hard-pressed inky lines, abrupt starts and stops. Nick's distress was visible in every stroke. Cassie read it over, and over again.

Nick woke to her still analyzing its contents, absorbing each and every detail. "What does it say?" he asked groggily, wiping the sleep from his eyes.

"We need a personal item from each of our friends,"

Cassie said, turning to him. "Something that'll contain some of their energy or essence."

She looked around her bedroom as Nick threw off the covers and stood up. In her closet, she found the hoodie Adam had left at her house, and in her jewelry box was a pair of gold hoop earrings Diana had recently let her borrow.

"That's a start," she said, placing the two items side by side on her bed, in the center of the Nick-shaped indentation lingering on the sheets. "But how will we find stuff from everyone else?"

Then she remembered everything that had been left in the basement when her friends were all sleeping there.

"The secret room," Nick said, sharing the thought with her.

The two of them hurried downstairs to rummage through their friends' belongings. They tore through the room, pulling at every drawer and opening every closet, tossing useless finds aside and out of the way.

Nick found a pair of Sean's sneakers, Doug's skateboard, and Chris's baseball cap. Cassie grabbed Deborah's motorcycle helmet, Laurel's favorite scarf, and a pair of Melanie's eyeglasses.

Then Nick held up a satiny red thong. "I'm pretty sure this is Faye's," he said.

Cassie ripped it from Nick's hands, laughing. She couldn't help it. She was giddy. Their friends were as good as saved.

They stood over the great pile of stuff they'd accumulated, admiring it.

"Where should we perform the spell?" Nick asked.

Cassie reached into her pocket and unfolded Nick's translation. "It says here it should be performed at the point of origin. What do you think that means?"

"Maybe where the possession took place," Nick said. "That would be the caves."

Cassie agreed. The remote caves where all this began seemed like an appropriate location.

"Do you think we should bring Max?" Cassie asked. "Someone besides us should be there in case something goes wrong. Though the caves are probably the last place he wants to see again."

"He might say no, but we should ask him." Nick gathered their friends' belongings into his arms to carry upstairs. "I'll go over to his house and talk to him about it while you gather the rest of the materials."

Cassie felt her chest fill with hope. "We make quite the pair," she said.

"The daughter of an evil witch," Nick said, smiling. "And a half-possessed screwup."

"The dream team," Cassie laughed.

~~~~~~~~~~

That evening, Cassie, Nick, and Max rowed through the dark, out to the caves. Max wanted to come. He'd told Nick he felt it was his duty to see the demons' destruction through—after all, they were his father's true murderers.

Nick docked the boat, tying it with thick rope to a protruding stump. He and Cassie entered the cave, with Max following close behind. They got right to work, solemnly preparing the spell. But the strange energy of the space didn't go unnoticed. So much had happened there. Max stood over the spot where his father had lain dead. His shoulders seemed to fold in on themselves; his head hung down listlessly.

Cassie went to him. "You can wait outside by the boat," she said. "It means a lot that you're here, but I know this must be painful for you."

"It's not only that," Max said. The hard dirt of the cave floor shuffled loudly beneath his feet. "Do you really think they'll be saved?"

"I hope so." When Max remained quiet she added, "Don't you?"

"Of course," he said immediately. "I want Diana to be okay." Then he lowered his voice. "I just don't know if I'm ready to see her again, to have her be back for real."

Cassie glanced at Nick preparing the spell. "In all honesty, I feel the same way about Adam. I'm nervous to face him after . . ." She paused. "After all that's happened."

Max appeared surprised by this.

"Nobody's relationship is perfect," Cassie clarified. "No matter how it appears on the outside."

"But the cord," Max said. "It's supposed to be this bond that overcomes everything. We're supposed to be soul mates. But I'm still so—" He stopped himself.

"Angry," Cassie said. "Hurt, confused. It makes sense for you to feel all of that."

She reached for Max's hand and squeezed it. "Adam's my soul mate, but his love for me wasn't strong enough to break through the possession. In fact, he's been with Scarlett all this time. You know how that makes me feel?"

Max shook his head. "I can't imagine."

"The cord begins the bond, Max. But it's something you have to work on."

"Everything's in place," Nick interrupted, blowing out a match.

Max was still holding Cassie's hand. "You know what, Cassie?" he said. "You're alright."

"Feeling's mutual," she said.

Nick brought Cassie the Master Tools—the bracelet, the garter, and the diadem—and she put them on. Max took a step back, and Nick entered into the circle with everyone's stuff.

Cassie lit the final four candles, one at each compass point, and closed the circle with her dagger. She stood at the northernmost point. The only sound aside from their breathing was the whistle of wind from the cave's mouth.

Cassie shut her eyes and began to chant. Once she felt like her energy was balanced, she started reciting the words of the exorcism.

Mando vobis, spiritus, quicumque es, et omnes clientes tui inferri haec corpora migrare.

She opened her eyes to let her gaze pass over Nick and the items belonging to her friends. She could see the spirit and energy contained in each item as a hovering color. All the items together created a multicolored cloud.

Litteris mando tibi me servire. Minister sum bonorum.

Cassie raised her hands over the pile and called out, "*Recesserimus adverse potentiae.*"

Then she dug her hand into a bowl of salt Nick had prepared. She filled her fist with its fine translucent grains, then sprinkled them over the pile of her friends' belongings and upon Nick's head.

Eicio a daemone amici. Purgátæ sis salis per salutem corporis et animae sanitatem. Omne malum quod te colit omnis malitia et astutia, qua te longe repellantur.

Next Cassie dipped her hands into a bowl of water. She sprinkled its droplets over the pile just as she did with the salt.

Eicio a daemone amici. Mundata sitis aqua vi fugant potestatem hostium excidere ex animo amoveas malis.

She raised both her arms up in a V and called out in a confident voice, "*Discedere, malum spiritus. Exi, seductor. Relinquere haec innocens corpora. Abire!*"

Cassie bowed, closing her eyes. A surge of energy

welled up in her chest. It spilled over and flooded her veins with an icy hot rush. She strove to maintain her footing, to not cry out. But this gushing energy was more than she could bear—she had to succumb to it, falling to her knees with a desperate gasp.

When she reopened her eyes, she felt better, empowered, almost blissful. She thought she sensed a change in the air, but only Nick would know for sure.

"How do you feel?" she asked him, rising back to her feet.

He looked at Cassie and at Max, who were watching him carefully. "I'm not sure."

"Try accessing the demon," Cassie said.

Reluctantly, Nick closed his eyes for a moment and went inward. It only took a few seconds for the slithering things to show themselves on his neck.

"Whoa!" Max yelled. "Okay, stop."

Cassie quickly dropped down to wrap her arm around Nick's shoulders. "Stop," she said. "We failed."

Nick breathed deeply until he was back to himself.

"What could have gone wrong?" Max asked.

Cassie removed the diadem from her head, as well as the bracelet and the garter. "I don't know," she said. "I felt like it was working, but I couldn't maintain it. It was too much."

"You need help," Nick said. "This spell is too powerful to perform on your own."

"What about your mom?" Max suggested.

Cassie shook her head. "Too risky. And my mother's magic isn't . . ."

She trailed off and Nick finished her sentence for her. "It isn't Blak magic."

"Which only leaves one person strong enough to help me," Cassie said.

Max looked at both of them, unsure what they were getting at.

"Scarlett," Nick said. "You need Scarlett's dark magic."

CHAPTER 12

It was just after dawn, and Cassie was walking along the beach, thinking of everything and nothing at once. She climbed up the bluffs and over the dunes, getting pebbles in her shoes, until she found a soft patch of sand free from driftwood and beach grass. She sat, pulled her knees up, and took a breath of salty air. The ocean roared in front of her.

What could be worse than needing someone you couldn't stand, someone you literally never wanted to see again? It made Cassie sick to her stomach. If all of Cassie's problems could be embodied in one person, it would be Scarlett: She'd brought havoc and dark magic to Cassie's

Circle; she knew Cassie's friends would be possessed by performing the hunter curse and allowed it to happen; not least of all, she'd managed to steal Cassie's boyfriend—for now. But Nick was right. Cassie had to get Scarlett on her side. As much as she hated to admit it, she *needed* her.

If Cassie couldn't perform the exorcism successfully by the full moon, her friends would be lost to her forever. And so would Adam.

Cassie let the memory of her failed attempt at the exorcism wash over her. It was a terrible disappointment, but alone here on the beach she could admit something else—she'd felt a flash of relief at the failure.

Of course she wanted Adam back. But what would it actually feel like now to have him return? What if she felt nothing at all?

First save him, and then address the state of their relationship, she told herself.

That afternoon Cassie headed to the abandoned warehouse where Scarlett was staying. The warehouse she swore she'd never step foot in. Scarlett was right about one thing: Never say never.

It was too risky to bring Nick to a place that was swarming with ancestor spirits. As strong as she knew he was, and as much as she feared being there alone, it would be reckless to deliver him to them that way. It took some convincing, but eventually Nick agreed.

The building was a fifteen-minute walk down the coast. Everyone in town casually referred to it as "the warehouse," but it was actually an old naval base that had been closed in the late 1980s. The main floor had been used as barracks to house soldiers and military families. Some of the upper floors were used to store weapons. And a section toward the back of the building, below ground, was known as the Bomb Wing. It had been used for raids and drills.

Cassie had heard stories about this place since she first moved to New Salem—scary stories, in fact—but she'd never believed them or experienced them herself. There were tales that the warehouse was haunted by evil spirits, the ghosts of fallen soldiers. Neighborhood children dared one another to knock on the windows without running away. Cassie had the urge to run away now as she crossed onto the property. She knew that the building was indeed haunted, not by ghost soldiers, but by the Blaks.

From the front, the multistory building looked like a run-down industrial factory. Most of the windows were boarded up, and its exterior was dotted with rusty metal signs that read: U.S. GOVERNMENT PROPERTY, NO TRESPASSING.

Vandals had spray-painted over many of them with rainbowed graffiti tags, pictures, and the occasional political statement.

Cassie approached the main entrance's corroded door, and Scarlett slid it open before she even had the chance to knock.

"To what do I owe this pleasure?" Scarlett asked.

"We need to talk," Cassie said.

"I knew you'd come around." Scarlett gestured for Cassie to enter.

Cautiously, Cassie stepped over the rickety threshold that reminded her of a barn door. Inside, the warehouse looked almost like a movie set, a backdrop to a film about World War II or Vietnam. Camouflage jackets hung on hooks, helmets above, jungle boots below. There was weaponry everywhere and an odor of metal and dirt. At any moment, Cassie believed, a whistle-blowing drill sergeant might storm the set, calling for attention. After nearly thirty years of this building being abandoned, standing in it now felt like traveling back in time. It was amazing that it had never been looted, perhaps because everyone who visited here recognized its rare timeless quality.

Chris, Sean, and Doug appeared from the shadows.

They gathered around Cassie, up on the balls of their feet, their fingers spread. Cassie steeled herself for whatever spell they were ready to hurl her way.

"Leave us alone!" Scarlett commanded.

Then Diana called to them from upstairs, snapping them to attention. Cassie could see her standing at the top of the stairwell.

They lowered their arms, deflated, and made their way up the steps. Cassie checked every shadow and corner. There was no sign of Adam.

Scarlett waited for Chris, Sean, and Doug—and Diana—to fully disappear before inviting Cassie to join her in a makeshift living room. They sat across from each other on drab green military cots, opposite a metal ammunition box that served as a coffee table. Kerosene lanterns propped up on rusted crates provided the only source of light.

Cassie looked up and all around the vast mildewed room. Old paint chipped from the walls in broken, musty shards. The air was stuffy and stale, though the ceilings were high. Cassie felt a damp chill. This was a dismal place, and she didn't want to be here a moment longer than necessary.

"I'll get right to the point," she said, edging forward

to the corner of her rank cot. "You've won, Scarlett. I'm done."

Scarlett's lips cracked slightly into a smile and her dark eyes widened, but Cassie could see she was doing her best not to reveal too much emotion. "Continue," she said. "I trust there's more."

"I've come to offer you a trade," Cassie said.

Cassie glanced at each corner of the warehouse floor to check for spying spirits, but she saw none. Still, she couldn't help but feel like she was being watched.

"I'll trade you Black John's Book of Shadows," she whispered, "in exchange for your help in exorcising the Circle."

Scarlett's face brightened, but she still appeared dubious. "You must be joking."

"I've translated most of the book at this point anyway," Cassie continued in a hushed tone. "And it's brought me so much trouble, I want nothing more to do with it."

"But giving it to me could unleash hell," Scarlett said. "You understand that. So what's the trick?"

"No trick. All I want is to save my friends."

"So let me get this straight," Scarlett said. "You're willing to sell out the entire world for *friendship*." She uttered the last word like it was a disease.

"Yes," Cassie said. She knew this was a dangerous deal, but she was desperate. And she had a plan to get the book back once her friends were on her side again. For now, she had to take it one step at a time.

"I just need your help to properly perform the exorcism," Cassie said. "I can't do it without you."

"You're serious." Scarlett finally allowed herself to laugh out loud. "You're even weaker than I thought."

Cassie rested her hands on the rough green wool of her cot's blanket. Its coarse fibers pinched the surface of her palms like tiny slivers of glass.

"No wonder Adam was bored by you," Scarlett said.

Cassie made no reaction. She wouldn't give Scarlett that satisfaction.

"You've got yourself a deal," Scarlett said finally.

Cassie eyed her warily. For once it appeared that Scarlett didn't have an angle. It must be in her best interest to be rid of the ancestors.

"I said I'll do it." Scarlett raised her voice. "I'm agreeing to what you want; the least you can do is say thank you."

"I'll want to do it right away," Cassie said. "The text of the spell called for performing it at the point of origin. So we should meet at the caves."

Scarlett shook her head. "The point of origin would

mean the place the spirits rose from. That would be the old cemetery, where many of their bodies were buried. And where our father is."

Cassie remained quiet for a few seconds. This was another reason she needed Scarlett's help. She was simply *good* at this kind of thing.

For a moment Cassie wondered if having the wrong location was the reason the spell didn't work before, but it was already too late to go back on the deal.

"I'll gather the Circle tonight," Scarlett said. "At midnight, near our father's crypt. We'll need to harness as much of our family energy as possible if this is going to work. The crypt is the best place."

"How will you get them to the cemetery?" Cassie asked.

"I'll tell them I got one of you to cross over, that we're performing a binding spell to complete the Circle." Scarlett stood up and signaled for Cassie to do the same.

She led Cassie to the door by the arm. "Are you sure you've really figured out the text to the exorcism spell?" she asked. "It's a tough spell to get right."

What was it that Cassie was hearing in Scarlett's tone? Mockery? Condescension?

No matter. There wasn't time to worry about Scarlett's

mind games. Once her friends were saved, she'd deal with Scarlett.

"I've got it covered," Cassie said.

She continued forward and out the sliding door. The bright afternoon sun struck her eyes as a surprise, and the gust of fresh air was welcome.

"I'll see you at midnight," she said to Scarlett, trying to sound unafraid. But she didn't slow her pace away from the warehouse's shadow until she was halfway down the sun-kissed block.

CHAPTER 13

It was ten minutes till midnight. Cassie, Nick, and Max were walking to the old cemetery, along Crowhaven Road. Nick carried a giant duffel bag over his shoulder filled with the belongings of their friends. Cassie carried the rest of the supplies they'd need to re-perform the exorcism.

Max pushed open the wrought-iron gate that led to the cemetery grounds, but then hesitated, looking like he couldn't bear to step through. He glanced at Cassie and then down at his shoes. "We just buried him here," he said, meaning his father.

Nick put his hand on Max's shoulder. "Why not let us handle this on our own?"

"Because I want to be there to see these ancestors go down," Max said. "They tried to burn me to death with the rest of the school, remember?"

"I know," Nick said, backing off slightly. "Then why not watch from here? It'll be safer, for Cassie and me, in case anything goes wrong. You won't be able to help anybody from the middle of it all."

Max considered this and after a moment agreed. "Good luck," he said.

Cassie and Nick continued through the gate, but they only walked a few feet when Nick also came to a halt.

"What's wrong?" Cassie asked. "Did we forget something?"

"No, we've remembered everything." Nick slid the tip of his boot back and forth in an arc across the crunchy gravel path. "It's going to work this time, I can feel it. This'll all be over soon," he said, without qualifying what exactly he meant by *this*.

Cassie knew what Nick was getting at: that she would soon be reunited with Adam.

She exhaled deeply, unsure what to say.

Nick reached out and took Cassie by the arms. "Not everything has to automatically go back to the way it was before," he said. "You have choices."

Cassie could see the love in his eyes. But what could she do? Adam was her soul mate. "One thing at a time," she said, taking his hand. "Come on."

Walking across the soft, uneven grass brought an instant flood of awful memories. So many of Cassie's loved ones had died recently—her grandmother, Melanie's great-aunt Constance, Suzan. Their faces, both alive and dead, all came back to her now.

She and Nick marched straight down the middle row, which bisected the cemetery grounds, lined on both sides with stone arches. Some of the monuments were cracked like broken teeth. Others were white and solid as bleached bones. Cassie tried to avoid looking at the ones that were crudely etched with skulls and ominous images. The grim reaper had been carved into more than one.

When I die, Cassie thought, *I want a much more pleasant figure on my headstone.* When *I die.* Not *if*, but when. This was what coming to the cemetery always reminded her—that life was precious but finite, that one day she would be dead.

Nick wrapped his free arm around Cassie's shoulders, and she leaned into his hold.

Scarlett and the Circle were waiting just where Scarlett had said they'd be. Under the moon they appeared like ghosts swaying in the wind around Black John's crypt.

Cassie could barely look at the colossal stone chamber of his burial vault. The hairs on the back of her neck tingled as she and Nick came upon it. She hugged her father's book to her chest—a moment later she would be handing it over to Scarlett.

Gaslight lanterns provided extra light, which flickered across Scarlett's face, not unlike the way it had in the warehouse. Cassie saw that a circle had already been drawn into the ground and her friends were standing within it, waiting for her.

Diana, Adam, and Faye came to attention at the sight of the book, but otherwise they remained still. It appeared that Scarlett had cast a spell freezing them in place.

Cassie joined Scarlett in the center. Nick emptied the duffel bag of their friends' belongings onto the ground and arranged them into a neat pile beside Cassie and Scarlett. He worked quickly, lighting the necessary incense and candles with his Zippo. When all was set, he took his place on the circle with the others.

He gave Cassie a reassuring nod and, finally, a smile.

Scarlett closed the circle on the ground with her silver-handled knife.

Cassie lifted her father's book with quivering hands and held it out to Scarlett.

Dropping her knife on the ground, Scarlett accepted the book. "Let's do this," she said.

Cassie exhaled a breath of relief. Scarlett must have been satisfied enough to have the book to herself to keep up her end of the bargain.

Cassie and Scarlett linked hands to meld their energy. Cassie scanned the faces of each of her friends. It appeared they truly believed they were about to perform a binding spell for a full Circle. Their enthusiasm was palpable.

Together, Cassie and Scarlett began the exorcism spell exactly as Cassie had done on her own at the caves. They recited the chants and performed the purifying rituals with the salt, and then with the water. But this time there was a quivering excitement within Cassie's chest, a tingling in her legs. The energy Cassie felt coursing through her body was double what it was last time she performed the spell.

Cassie got the sense that she was rising, swirling, higher and higher. It was a dark feeling, there was no doubt about that; it was thick with power, equal parts pain and bliss. Her breath came quickly.

She forced her eyes open to watch the effect on her friends. They appeared just as overcome by the incredible force of the spell as she was. She could see the darkness pouring out of their eyes like tears, and their mouths, like blood. It ran down their chins, their necks and chests, down the insides of their legs, until it seeped into the moist dirt.

Cassie and Scarlett raised their arms up in a V and called out the final incantation in their strongest voices: *"Discedere, malum spiritus. Exi, seductor. Relinquere haec innocens corpora. Abire!"*

Cassie could see the black shadows within her friends rise up and out of their bodies like smoke, coiling, wheeling. The spirits were breaking free, she was sure of it. Cassie felt their energy rush over her head and past her sides, cold and dark and quick, in an icy, deathlike *whoosh*.

Cassie heard herself scream. She'd flown backward, and found herself on the ground.

She lay flat there, still for a moment, gazing at the starless midnight sky. Her head was spinning. Her bones ached. Shakily, she sat up and refocused her vision.

As her sight sharpened, she recognized what had come into view. She was seeing Adam's eyes looking back at her. They were the truest, most beautiful blue she had ever seen—the color of the ocean at its most radiant. The rest of his face was the same as ever: arresting and kind, with pride showing in his high cheekbones and determined mouth.

"Cassie," he said, like an apology.

He wrapped himself around her, and his heart beat evenly and steady against her chest. She'd never felt so thankful for anything in all her life.

From the moment their eyes met, neither of them could turn away. The world had gone still, and only the two of them remained. It wasn't possible to squeeze his body close enough.

He kissed her on her trembling mouth, and she was swept away.

When she returned to her surroundings, a little dazed, she noticed that the whole group had climbed to their feet.

The gentle composure of Diana's features had returned. Melanie's cool strength reentered the sharp angles of her face. And Laurel's pixielike air had settled back into her smile. Faye ran her hands down her neck and torso, feeling herself returned. Cassie looked at each of her friends, finding that every one of them had come back to being the person she loved.

They were saved.

Cassie glanced at the cemetery gate and caught sight

of Max walking away. He'd seen enough, Cassie assumed. All he could manage for now.

Adam wrapped himself around Cassie again. She breathed him in, not even realizing how much she'd missed the little things about him, like the smell of his skin and the feel of his hand flat upon her back. Now that he had returned, she felt the full force of the loss of him. It was like a dream to be in his arms again, too good to be true.

Then she glanced at Nick.

He tried to force a smile at her before looking away.

Cassie felt a pang of guilt. In her heart she knew getting Adam back had come at the expense of what she'd had with Nick, but this moment was too powerful to be spoiled, too perfect.

As Nick continued staring straight down at the ground, Cassie wanted to go to him, to scream out, *We did it!* But she couldn't.

Adam was holding her so tightly now. He rested his chin on top of Cassie's head the way he always used to do. He spoke in a quiet, sorrowful voice.

"I was in there the whole time," he said. "I was screaming at this spirit to stop. That he was hurting you, Cassie . . ."

"I know," Cassie said. "It wasn't your fault."

"I'm just so glad you're okay." He held Cassie tighter. "I wanted to come through for you, but I just couldn't. The demon was too strong."

Diana and the others then entered into the fold of Cassie and Adam's hug. But Nick stayed to the outside. It was a bittersweet moment. She wanted him near her, too.

Scarlett, Cassie realized, was also keeping to herself, not rejoicing in the least.

Cassie called to her. "Get in here! We couldn't have done this without you!"

But Scarlett made no motion toward the group. She stared at them oddly and then glanced upward.

The sky above the cemetery had filled with storm clouds. Ravens flocked from the nearby trees, and the resident stray cats fled. Cassie felt her relief tiptoe away, replaced by a tightening, choking fear.

There was movement in the shadows around them, a stirring of shrubs. Cassie realized they were not alone. Footsteps and dim shapes approached them, and she could hear the sound of breath—of breathing. Then Cassie noticed a wicked grin sneak onto Scarlett's face.

CHAPTER 14

Figures emerged from the shadows around the Circle, creeping out from behind the cover of trees and tombstones. Cassie could see they were bodies. People. And they were wearing ancient garb that was half-rotted away. Cassie watched them and shuddered, understanding immediately that these were the demons that had possessed her friends for the past week, returned to their corporeal form. Her ancestors had been truly resurrected now.

Cassie stayed close to her Circle. Instinctively, they packed in tightly to one another as a unit. They all knew. Adam reached for Cassie's hand.

Cassie turned to Scarlett, who smiled with the

satisfaction of someone who has had the pleasure of watching her plan unfold perfectly.

"Scarlett was one step ahead of us the whole time," Nick whispered. "Again."

"What can we do?" Deborah let out a heavy breath. "We don't even know if they're dead or alive."

"They look pretty alive to me," Laurel said.

As the figures of Cassie's long-dead ancestors grew nearer, she thought back to all that Timothy had told her about these relatives. She recognized Black John's sister, Alice, immediately. The rope burn from her hanging in the witch trials had chafed and bruised a chokerlike ring across her throat. Other than that, she looked just like she did in the drawing, but slighter and with even gloomier eyes. Her pain was more palpable in three-dimensional form than it was on paper. She may have been the saddest girl Cassie had ever seen.

"I say we run," Sean said. "Get out of here while we have the chance."

Diana was eyeing Alice with a fearful curiosity. "No," she said. "We have to stand our ground."

Cassie lost track of Scarlett in the approaching crowd, but she recognized another ancestor—the man Timothy had said lived his life as a priest corrupting the Church. Absolom. He was the one who had copied the forbidden text of the exorcism rite into the Book of Shadows, and Cassie knew he was the ancestor who had possessed Adam.

Absolom appeared younger than he was in the drawing Timothy had showed her, but she was sure it was him. He wore the black garb and white collar of a priest, and he stood with the posture of a man used to an audience.

Adam couldn't take his eyes off him. He was enraptured by Absolom's saintly yet demonic presence, his wickedness cloaked in righteousness.

"Don't show them any fear," Nick said. But all of Cassie's friends were trembling.

One of the female ancestors had drawn in close to Faye, sizing her up. Cassie could identify who she was most easily because she had been so badly burned. Beatrix. The flesh on her face and arms was browned and stiff, all mottled and blistered. Her hands were gruesomely charred, each finger reminding Cassie of burnt meat on a skewer. But even so, Cassie could see that Beatrix was beautiful. The shape of her nose and lips demanded attention despite their disfigurement, and she carried herself with confidence and grace, like a dancer. Her eyes and hair were so dark Cassie imagined they'd blackened to that gloomy hue in the fire that had consumed her.

Cassie surveyed the remaining ancestors, whom she didn't recognize. They ranged in age and appearance, but none were very old. Aside from the fact that life spans were shorter in the past, Cassie understood that most of her relatives had also been hunted and killed for being witches. Not one of them had passed forty years old, by the looks of them.

One of the male ancestors wiggled his dirty fingers and swung his mud-encrusted arms forward and back. He was dressed in the clothes of a peasant, or possibly a farmworker. Cassie recognized him from the album Timothy had given her. His name was Samuel, and he was from the Providence Plantation—one of the original thirteen colonies—which, after the American Revolution, became Rhode Island.

The woman standing nearest him was wearing a Civil War–era day dress with red and white stripes that would have been charming if it weren't half-decomposed. In the Blak family album she was described as a Southern belle: Charlotte Blak of Louisville, Kentucky.

Another man, whom Cassie recognized as Thomas Blak from England in the seventeenth century, wore a torn gray riding habit with matching breeches. He took off his hat and examined it.

But it was Alice who most captivated Cassie. She could hardly take her eyes off Alice's pouty-lipped scowl. And she noticed that Alice had the same effect on Diana. Timothy had warned Cassie not to be fooled by Alice's looks. He'd told her that Alice was so obsessed with dark magic that some said she was more evil than Black John himself. But now that Alice had appeared in the flesh, with her heartbreaking gaze and her longing, with her girlish hair nestled into a braided bun, Cassie felt like she understood her—who she *really* was.

"It's good to be back," Alice said. Her voice was startlingly deep. It was a voice vacant of all emotion, concave, as if Alice herself believed her words to be utterly worthless even as she said them.

"Better than good," Absolom announced, with a cadence that thundered over the group. He spoke with an accent Cassie couldn't decipher. "Triumphant."

Beatrix nodded. Her face cracked into a distasteful grin. "This town is ours for the taking," she said. She raised her burned hands and aimed them at Cassie and her friends, poised to cast a spell.

"Not yet," Alice said, stepping between Beatrix and

the Circle. She rested her terrible eyes on Cassie. "First we get stronger."

Scarlett emerged from the back of the crowd then, shoving her way to the front. "I can help," she said. "I've prepared a place for us."

Beatrix eyed Scarlett like she was a fly to be shooed. "Can I at least destroy this one?" she asked Alice.

Alice shook her head. "Show us this place," she said to Scarlett, and then she positioned her thin hand on Beatrix's back. "We'll destroy them all in good time."

Adam took a step forward, as if he were preparing to fight them.

"No," Cassie said, pulling him back.

She tried to keep her Circle corralled behind her as Alice and the others retreated to wherever Scarlett was leading them.

"We can't just let them go," Adam said.

"Conant's right," Nick said. "They're weak right now; this might be our only chance."

"You're all weak right now, too," Cassie said. "And so am I after performing that spell."

She looked around at the surrounding graves and headstones with their skulls and grim reaper etchings, and then at her father's massive chambered crypt. She looked into the faces of her dear friends, thankfully returned to her, and at the backs of her resurrected ancestors in the distance. "We'll have our chance to fight them," Cassie said. "This is only the beginning."

CHAPTER 15

The Circle walked straight to Cassie's house, barely talking.
Maybe they were traumatized, or just exhausted. Cassie
held Adam's hand, but much of the joy from their ini-
tial embrace had vanished. Once again triumph had led
immediately to setback, this one possibly far worse than
the first.

But it was a minor victory not lost on Cassie when
each of her friends was able to cross the property line to
her house unhindered. Cassie hadn't been sure she'd ever
see that wish realized. She glanced at Nick to share in the
appreciation of the small blessing, and he half-smiled in
response.

The group congregated in Cassie's living room, and it was just like old times, everyone lying about. Adam hovered close to Cassie on the couch—but for a change, Nick wasn't keeping a little off to the side. He sat down right beside Cassie, sandwiching her between himself and Adam.

"I'm going to text Max," Nick said. "He deserves to know what's going on."

"You two have become friends?" Diana blurted out.

Cassie offered Diana a reassuring glance.

"Would he really come here?" Diana asked. "I wouldn't blame him if he never wanted to see me again."

"He's been really helpful these past few days," Nick said, without looking up from his phone.

"But he may not be ready to forgive the rest of us," Diana said. "Me especially."

Cassie feared Diana might be right. Max was still feeling torn. Cassie understood how that felt, with Adam on one side of her and Nick on the other.

No sooner had Cassie come to this conclusion than there was a knock at the door. Diana straightened her posture at the sound.

"It's Max," Cassie said, recognizing his light brown hair and lacrosse jacket through the window. She opened the door and invited him in. He stood stiffly in the doorway, eyeing the group before taking the first step toward them. Nobody spoke. Everyone in the Circle was watching Diana, and Diana was watching Max.

"Hi," was all he said. It was the shortest, most non-committal word he could have offered Diana, but it was something. Diana rose from where she was seated but restrained herself from running to him.

Max's eyes filled with emotion. He looked at her now with a long, measured glance. The goodness and purity that shone back at him from Diana was undeniable.

Max took another careful step forward and slightly opened his arms.

Diana nearly collapsed into his embrace. The air around them crackled with electricity. Cassie could feel their connection as if it were her own with Adam. The whole group must have felt it, because everyone's shoulders settled and their jaws relaxed.

Max became conscious of his audience. He blushed and looked at Cassie and Nick. "So I guess it's safe to say the evil spirits are gone once and for all."

Nick let out a snort. "Nothing is ever that simple for us, unfortunately."

Diana led Max to an empty seat among the group. "The

THE TEMPTATION

spirits are out of our bodies," she said. "But now they're in their own, running around free in New Salem."

"And we need to figure out how to get rid of them," Cassie said, taking the floor. She looked at Nick specifically.

"While you were all possessed, the ancestors were insistent on getting the Book of Shadows," she said. "The book must be the key to it all."

Nick agreed. "If the book is what invited them back into the world," he said, "maybe it's the way to get them out."

Melanie and Laurel leaned forward. Sean, Chris, Doug, and Deborah were visibly plotting in their minds how they might use the book to thwart the dark ancestors' plot.

"Then let's go through the book right now," Faye said. "Analyze it until we figure out how to get rid of these bastards."

Cassie's friends had somehow overlooked the fact that she no longer had the book. They were all still possessed when she'd handed it over to Scarlett. The spell must have occupied all their attention.

Only Nick realized the truth. "Cassie can't go get the book right now," he said.

Adam wasn't used to being one step behind, especially when it concerned Cassie. "Why not?" he asked, frustrated.

Cassie dropped her eyes. "I gave the book to Scarlett. I traded it for her help with the exorcism spell."

A deadly silence washed over the room.

Cassie shrank beneath it, for having played so easily into Scarlett's plan. "I'm sorry," she said. "But it was the only way I knew how to get you all back."

There were attempts at encouraging nods all around, but the morale of the group had nosedived.

"Well then," Max said unexpectedly, catching the whole Circle off guard with his tone of cooperation. "The first item of business is to get the book back."

"Yes." Diana took Max's hand. She practically glowed. "That's exactly what we'll do."

~~~~~~~~~~

Cassie closed and locked the front door as the last of her friends left for the night.

"Alone at last," Adam said.

It was finally just the two of them, for the first time since he'd been himself again. Cassie took him by the hand and led him upstairs to her room.

She dropped onto her bed, and Adam joined her.

It suddenly occurred to her how exhausted she was. She couldn't get the sight of those wretched ancestors out of her mind. It left her with a weighty sense of dread, as if she'd swallowed a heavy stone and it had gotten lodged in her chest.

Adam let his hand fall on her leg and kept it there. "You're glad I'm back," he asked, "aren't you, Cassie?"

"Are you kidding? I never want to let you out of my sight."

Adam looked down at his hand, which he still hadn't moved. "I wish it had been me to help you these past few days, not Nick. It should have been me."

Cassie wondered if Adam remembered how close he'd gotten to Scarlett. Was that contributing to his shame?

"I don't want you to think it's because my love wasn't strong enough," Adam continued. "It wasn't that. It was that Absolom was too strong."

Cassie cuddled up to Adam, covering them both with her heavy cotton comforter. It sheltered them like a tent. "I do know that," she said, as much for her own benefit as for Adam's.

The pillow behind Cassie's head was soft, and her sheets smelled fresh and clean. Having Adam with her made everything better.

"I want things to go back to normal," Adam said. "Between you and me. And I'm willing to do whatever it takes."

"I want that, too." Cassie rested her head on his shoulder. "It's already starting to feel that way."

Adam pulled her in closer. "Good."

Cassie closed her eyes to draw out the moment, to listen to his breath and his heartbeat. It was a slow and steady rhythm now, and she found her own heart adjusted to match it. Their chests rose and fell together, perfectly and unconsciously synchronized.

They began to doze off that way, wrapped up in each other's arms, descending to restful sleep and sweet dreams.

CHAPTER 16

"Did you hear what happened at Old Town Hall?"

"I heard it was vandalized. And someone also broke into the history museum."

"The shopping mall, too. The police are saying it may have been a group of people. They aren't sure if all the incidents are related."

Cassie was in English class, eavesdropping on Sally Waltman's conversation with her friend Tina.

Sally shot Cassie a knowing look when she realized she'd been listening. Cassie returned the gaze and then politely looked away.

These stories of robbery and vandalism weren't unique,

unfortunately. Cassie had been hearing about similar strange things happening around town in the last few hours. The ancestor witches were creating havoc all over New Salem now that they had their bodies back. Cassie kept a mental list of it all, and she feared the worst: that the ancestors were seeking retribution for all they'd lost in their lifetimes, all that had been taken from them by Outsiders.

After the bell rang, Cassie approached Sally as she was packing up her books. "I couldn't help but overhear," she said.

Sally scanned the surrounding area to be sure nobody was listening. "I knew something was up when your friends attacked me and ambushed the auditorium, but now it seems like the trouble is spreading into town. What's going on?"

"It's a long story," Cassie said.

"It is witch-related, isn't it?"

"Ancient witches," Cassie said as the two of them exited their classroom. "The worst in history."

They reached Cassie's locker. She opened it to exchange her English notebook for her math textbook. "I'm afraid what they're after is revenge—on New Salem, on the whole world."

"On Outsiders," Sally added.

"You can be sure of that." Cassie slammed her locker shut. "Even before they were killed, they wanted to destroy all non-witches. Now they have their own untimely deaths to avenge."

"Is there anything I can do to help?" Sally asked.

The offer warmed Cassie's heart. If only her ancestors had encountered Outsiders so willing to set aside their differences, they might not be so quick to judge.

"Thank you," Cassie said. "I'll let you know. For now, keep your eyes open, and be careful."

Cassie turned around to make her way to her next class, and she came face-to-face with Alice.

She gasped.

"Sally, I'll see you later," Cassie said, and Sally had the good sense to walk away.

Black John's sister still had a sadness about her, but she looked different from the last time Cassie had seen her. She'd let down her dark brown hair, and Cassie noticed it had been cut into layers. Her blue-gray eyes were subtly etched with liner, and her eyebrows had been plucked to a cleanly lined arch. She wore tight jeans, a sheer black blouse, and about a dozen necklaces of various sizes and styles, probably to cover the mark on her neck. She looked good, Cassie thought, and a second later the deeper truth sunk in: She looked *modern*.

So that's what the ancestors were doing at the mall. They'd gone on a shopping spree and given themselves makeovers.

Lurking behind Alice was the other ancestor who was young enough to easily pass as a student: Beatrix. She had also updated her look to blend in unnoticed at school, but more shockingly, she no longer appeared burned. She must have done a spell to heal her mottled skin, because it shimmered in a way Cassie could only describe as magical. Her face was pale and smooth and new, untouched by her difficult life.

Alice blinked her cheerless eyes at Cassie. "Niece," she said.

Her voice startled Cassie just as it did the first time she heard it. It reminded Cassie of the way her own voice had sounded when she had strep throat. She remembered how it felt like someone was stabbing her in the tonsils every time she tried to utter a word.

Cassie unconsciously brought her hand up to her own neck. She swallowed carefully.

Alice reached out to her, but Cassie took a step back, suddenly repulsed by the idea of this body—practically a living corpse—touching her.

Alice wrinkled her eyes, seeming hurt by Cassie's aversion.

"I want nothing to do with you," Cassie said, her voice cracking. Before she even realized what she was doing, she took aim at Alice and Beatrix and called out a spell: "*Infirmitate super vos!*"

Alice deflected Cassie's magic with a leisurely wave of her hand. "See," she said. "Now that's the Blak spirit."

Cassie's own surprise at casting that spell wasn't lost on Alice.

"Those instincts of yours," she said. "Don't you feel it? You're with us. You're one of the greats."

She exchanged a side glance with Beatrix. "We need a twelfth member to our Circle, Cassie. And we want that member to be you."

Cassie considered this. Was she one of them regardless of how hard she tried not to be? So many people, loved ones, had died on her watch as she'd striven to be good. And she was the one who performed the spell that released them into the world in the first place. She'd resurrected their evil, willingly or not.

The thought of it made Cassie sick. The urge to cast another dark spell at them was overwhelming.

"You'll never have me," Cassie said, fighting off her baser impulse.

A flush of anger crossed Alice's face, and Cassie was shocked at how quickly her expression could change from hurt to raw rage. "You think quite highly of yourself, don't you? Good. You should. But you can't resist your destiny."

"My Circle is my destiny," Cassie said. But her self-assurance was immediately overshadowed by another thought: *What about the rest of her friends?* The ancestors wanted Cassie, but if they couldn't get her, they'd just try for someone else. And they'd keep trying until they—

"Forget her," Beatrix said to Alice. "Every family has a weak link."

"She isn't weak," Alice snapped back.

It occurred to Cassie that the other ancestors might already be going after the members of her Circle—at this very moment. She didn't have time for this standoff with Alice and Beatrix.

Cassie turned on her heels and left them standing there. Let them think her a coward if they wanted to. She didn't care. She needed to find her friends, and fast.

———

Cassie texted the entire Circle: Emergency meeting. Meet at the Colony Diner ASAP!

The Colony Diner was just off school grounds. Close enough to walk to within minutes, but far enough away to be private and protected. Cassie arrived first and sat alone for a few minutes, tapping her fingernails on the orangey-yellow faux wood table. She ordered a strawberry milkshake to keep the waitress occupied. With each second that passed, the knot in her stomach tightened. What if none of them came? What if she'd already lost them?

But Adam arrived within minutes, then Diana, and finally Cassie calmed down enough to take a sip of her shake. Nick, Deborah, and Faye had been in the middle of Phys. Ed together, their least favorite class, so they were quick to cut out and make their way to the diner.

Melanie and Laurel appeared next, from study hall at the library, with overstuffed book bags weighing down their shoulders.

"What's the emergency?" Melanie asked.

"Has anyone heard from Sean, Chris, or Doug?" Cassie asked. It was no secret those three were all on the impressionable side. Some might even call them reckless.

Just after placing a food order with the waitress, Cassie caught sight of Chris's Jeep zipping into the parking lot. It settled into a spot, and Sean and Doug jumped out of the backseat. Cassie's whole body relaxed as she watched them dash for the diner's entrance.

"Sorry we're late," Sean said, squeezing into the booth

beside Nick, with Chris and Doug behind him. "We were at the park."

"In the middle of the school day?" Melanie raised her eyebrows.

"Never mind that," Doug said. "What did we miss?"

Cassie pushed her milkshake away and cleared her throat. "Alice and Beatrix showed up at school today. They need a twelfth member for their dark Circle. Which means they're going to be coming for every one of you."

Cassie focused on Sean, Chris, and Doug, and then, finally, Faye. "They're going to corner you, try to manipulate your weaknesses."

The waitress arrived with their order just as Cassie's last words trickled into the air. She set down plate after greasy plate and over-full cups, leaving no portion of the tabletop uncovered. It gave the group a much-needed moment to process what Cassie had just told them.

Once the waitress stepped away, Diana spoke. "We have to stand strong," she said. "We have to be a united front."

"I think it's a given," Deborah said, reaching for the pickle off Melanie's plate. "Who here wants to side with the demons?" She waited dramatically for a hand to go up. When none did, she said, "I rest my case."

"You're missing the point," Adam said. "You may not want that now, but these spirits were in our bodies. They know every one of our weaknesses, our every dream and desire. They're experts at manipulation."

Sean shoved a french fry into his mouth. "Being able to perform dark magic *would* be pretty cool."

Nick smacked him on the shoulder, causing him to choke.

"I was kidding," Sean said, coughing. "Jeez."

"Not funny," Laurel said. "Everyone has to promise to have no contact with any of the ancestors. We can't give them the chance to tempt us."

"Why are you looking at me?" Faye asked.

It had been obvious that Laurel directed her statement at Faye, but she denied it.

"I said *everyone*," Laurel insisted.

"At this point," Melanie said, tapping the top of Laurel's hand with her own, "I think it's safe to say we're all committed to avoiding the ancestors. We'll just have to watch each other's backs to keep it that way, that's all."

Faye forked at her Caesar salad without looking up. "Fine," she said. "As long as the puritanical goody two-shoes of our group don't use that as an excuse to butt into my private life."

Laurel opened her mouth to defend herself, but no sound came out.

"Agreed," Diana said. "We'll watch each other while respecting one another's privacy." She passed a stern look over the group until they all showed their assent.

"Sounds like a good plan to me," Cassie said. But she was more worried than she let on. Faye's face had changed at the mention of dark magic. It was no secret that she'd always been jealous of Cassie's powers.

After they finished eating, and the group dispersed to make it to their next classes, Cassie took Adam and Diana aside.

"I think the three of us should go tonight to steal the book back from Scarlett," she whispered. "*Just* the three of us. I'm worried about exposing the others to the ancestors."

Adam nodded, and a look of trepidation crossed Diana's face. "How will we do it?" she asked.

"By any means necessary," Cassie said.

CHAPTER 17

It was a well-known New Salem fact that the old warehouse where Scarlett was staying had one window in the back that was large enough to crawl through. For years it had served as the entrance to secret rendezvous and underage keg parties. Tonight it would be Cassie, Adam, and Diana's way to the book.

Adam ran ahead of Cassie and Diana to make sure the window was still penetrable and unguarded. Cassie watched him fiddle with the half-rotten wooden board and slide it out of place. The gaping hole in the building's facade reminded her of a missing tooth.

"You're as good as in," Adam said. "Just wait for the diversion to make your move."

Adam and Diana left her there to sneak around to the front of the warehouse. Cassie wasn't supposed to climb into the window until her cue, but she couldn't help herself. She desperately wanted the few extra minutes to look around.

She silently lifted herself inside and eyed the surrounding space, mentally calling to the book, alerting it that she had arrived—that she'd come to take it back home. She knew the book would answer her call.

It only took a few seconds for Cassie to hear the voices coming from the warehouse's makeshift dining room. She recognized Scarlett's high shrill and Alice's oppressive monotone, as well as an ambient collage of tapping forks upon plates, and water glasses shifting.

Cassie inched toward their sounds and ducked behind some old metal containers to watch them for a few seconds. She was surprised by the portrait that spread before her eyes. Scarlett and all the ancestors were gathered around a circular table that was covered with fine foods: roasted chicken, baked potatoes, salad greens, and vegetables. They were enjoying a meal together, smiling, laughing, debating. They looked like a family, a happy family.

Charlotte sliced a loaf of corn bread into thick squares while Samuel doled out crisp-looking cobs of yellow corn.

"Those hunters you killed," Alice said, "were of the same bloodline as the ones who had me hanged at Salem. Just as your bloodline is the same as ours, Scarlett." She raised her glass. "True justice."

"That's what family's for," Scarlett said, clinking her glass to Alice's.

They all seemed so at ease with each other. Witnessing their interaction made Cassie wonder if this was what Scarlett had been longing for all along—the connection of a family. The thought made Cassie's own heart begin to beat more heavily.

"It's a shame about Cassie," Beatrix said to Alice. "She's a stubborn girl; I don't think there's any convincing her."

"But we still need a twelfth," Absolom said. "By the full moon. Otherwise we'll have to wait another whole month to perform the spell."

What spell? Cassie wondered.

Alice glumly set down her water glass. "I really wanted it to be Cassie," she said.

Cassie felt a lump form in her throat, and she was overcome with a grief she couldn't identify. From the Blak family album, she'd learned that Alice began her life trying to be good. It wasn't until she turned fifteen that she came into her full power and was overcome by her own dark magic. Then the curse Timothy spoke of got the best of her—it drove her to do awful things to the non-witches of Salem. A year later she was hanged.

Cassie couldn't help but see a little of herself in her young aunt; they were both the same age when they discovered their magic. And she sensed Alice also saw something of herself in Cassie.

"I just wouldn't be able to stand it," Scarlett said, "if we have to wait another whole month to perform the spell."

Cassie primed her ears to take in more. She needed to learn about this spell they were planning—but just then Adam and Diana's commotion from outside became audible.

"Ssh," Thomas said. "What was that?"

All the ancestors halted their talk and listened. Scarlett dashed for the front of the warehouse, and Alice followed just behind.

Scarlett slid the rusty door open. The ancestors gathered around it to an unexpected spectacle. Diana and Adam had conjured a brilliant sphere of light, like a planet or spinning disco ball in the sky. They recited a chant:

Dark spirits, look at this light, look not away, give no fight.

The ancestors were dazed, caught off guard. Their eyes widened to the hypnotic shimmering orb before them. They were mesmerized by it.

Cassie knew this was her cue to snatch the book. She raised her arms and whispered her call: *"Liber, libri exaudi me venire ad me."*

From across the warehouse she heard movement, and then a sound like a latch coming undone. She repeated her call again and waited with open hands.

The book showed itself to her. Freed from its hiding place, it hovered above an open metal chest.

"Venire ad me," Cassie said, and the book swiftly flew to her hands.

Cassie could see that Alice and Beatrix and a few of the stronger ancestors were beginning to resist Adam and Diana's conjuring. It couldn't be long before they harnessed enough energy to break their spell.

With the book safely in hand, Cassie ran back to the window. She'd almost made it through when Absolom dropped in front of her, like a bat from the ceiling. He was wearing his black clothes and priest's collar, and his face was twisted in a cruel sneer. He readied himself to cast a spell, and Cassie froze with terror.

"Give me the book," he said.

Then he turned and pointed at Adam and Diana, bursting their ball of light into thick black smoke.

Alice shook herself awake. Alert now to her surroundings, she locked eyes with Cassie and saw the book in her grasp.

She and Absolom simultaneously hurled a spell at Cassie, or at the book—it was difficult to tell which—because the book immediately heated in Cassie's arms. But it wasn't burning her. It was reacting. And whatever spells they had cast had no other effect.

The book suctioned itself to Cassie's chest. She clasped it close and sensed its attachment, its energy. The book, she felt, was empowering her like a battery.

Absolom's brow wrinkled with confusion. He tipped his head at an angle, unable to comprehend how his power was being deflected.

Alice and the other ancestors stood in similar disbelief.

"Run!" Cassie screamed out to Adam and Diana, suddenly understanding that the book wanted to be with her—that she would be able to safely escape with it in her arms, but they might be held captive.

Adam and Diana did as Cassie said. But the ancestors weren't concerned with them or their escape. They moved in on Cassie with blackened eyes. Samuel had his hands raised and stared, expressionless, at her. Charlotte and Thomas whispered evil chants beneath their breath. But nothing could touch her. The book acted as Cassie's shield.

"Just let her go," Scarlett called out to them. "She can have the dumb book. It doesn't matter anymore. We've got what we need."

The ancestors ignored Scarlett. Absolom attempted the same spell Cassie had used to bring the book to her arms, but coming from him they were just empty words.

The book wasn't leaving Cassie.

Beatrix screamed at the others, "Don't let her get away!"

But Cassie was quick to turn around and jump through the window, then sprint toward the road. A few paces ahead of her in the shadowy distance, she could see Adam and Diana running safely through the dark night toward home.

~~~~~~~~~~~~

Back on Crowhaven Road, Cassie, Adam, and Diana finally stopped running. "We're alright," Cassie said, trying to calm herself as much as them. "We're safe."

"Thanks to the book," Adam said, trying to catch his breath. "Otherwise we would have been finished."

Diana kneeled over with her hands on her knees, gasping for air. "But you did it, Cassie, you got it back!"

Cassie stuffed the still-warm book beneath her shirt, securing it under the belt around her waist. She wanted to feel victorious, but Scarlett's voice still echoed in her ears. The ancestors had already gotten what they needed from the book: whatever spell Absolom had mentioned during their dinner.

"But they're planning something," Cassie said. "By the next full moon. With or without the book."

Adam put his arm around Cassie, and she didn't resist him. "You should be proud of yourself," he said, trying to keep her morale up as best he could. "For today at least, we won."

Still, as the three of them continued the walk home, a sense of defeat descended upon them. Adam became lost in thought, kicking up pebbles with each step. Diana hopelessly watched the tranquil night sky. For Cassie, running away from a battle never felt good. Even if it was her only option, and even if she'd gotten what she wanted—it still didn't feel dignified.

Cowardly. That was how Alice or Beatrix would have described her retreat. *Shameful.*

Diana came to a stop when they reached the turnoff that led to Max's house. "I'm heading this way," she said.

Cassie offered her a grin. At least Diana had Max back

THE TEMPTATION

in her life, her one and only soul mate. That was one joy-
ful thing Cassie could focus on.

"You've earned it," Cassie said. "We'll regroup tomorrow and figure out our next move."

Diana trudged off alone, quickening her pace a bit,
Cassie noticed, but still watching the sky.

Adam took Cassie's hand and walked her the rest of
the way to her house. When they climbed up the porch
steps, Cassie invited him in, even though she didn't need
to. Neither of them had to say aloud that they, too, didn't
want to be alone.

Cassie led Adam right up to her room, closed the door,
and lay down on her bed.

"I've never seen Diana so head over heels for a boy
before," Adam said.

Cassie smirked. "Not even you?"

"Not even me." He laughed, pulling Cassie in for a kiss.

For some reason the silver cord flashed through
Cassie's mind—not the cord between her and Adam but
the one between Adam and Scarlett. The fear it instilled
in Cassie had been overshadowed lately by all the other
more immediate threats she faced, but it never ceased to
exist somewhere in the background.

Adam was still kissing her, and Cassie was kissing him

back, but her mind drifted to Nick, and the incessant questions began rolling in: How can you ever know for sure that you've found your one true love? Is there even such a thing, silver cords aside? Can you have more than one soul mate?

Adam pulled back a moment. "You okay?" he asked.

Cassie took his face into her hands.

For tonight, she had to push all the questions and anxiety out of her mind. There weren't always going to be clear answers. She had to accept that.

Gently, she drew Adam's face toward her own.

Sometimes bodies could communicate in a way language couldn't. Adam's mouth on Cassie's said all there was to say.

CHAPTER 18

Cassie climbed into Adam's car the next morning wishing he would drive them anywhere but school. She'd woken up exhausted, like she could sleep away the whole day and still be tired.

Adam reached affectionately for her hand. "I know," he said. "I'm kind of dreading this day too. There'll probably be a retaliation coming our way."

Cassie barely had the energy to respond. But that was exactly what she'd been thinking. The book was safely hidden in her house, where no demons could cross onto the property, but she and her friends were fair game—especially at school. And after being showed up yesterday, Cassie was sure the ancestors were primed to flaunt their power.

Adam let Cassie zone out for a few minutes and focused on the road, but when they were nearing the Cup, he slowed the car. "You want to stop for a quick coffee?"

"I already had some this morning," Cassie said.

"It looks like you could use another," Adam replied, and then he immediately backpedaled. "I meant that in the nicest way possible." He smiled weakly.

Cassie sighed and gazed out the window. "Okay," she said. "I guess it couldn't hurt."

Then she saw something that snapped her right awake. "Wait," she said. "Is that Faye? With Beatrix?"

Adam squinted his eyes until he spotted them. "We have to follow her," he said, jerking the steering wheel sharply to the right.

He parked the car, and they made their way to the coffee shop's alternate entrance, a side door from which they watched Faye and Beatrix get their drinks and search for a place to sit.

Cassie strained to hear their conversation, but the shop was loud and bustling with the morning rush. Faye and Beatrix found an empty table near the front, too far away for Adam and Cassie to make out anything they were discussing. Slowly she and Adam inched nearer, but it was no use.

Adam thought for a moment. "I have an idea," he said. "An eavesdropping spell."

Cassie hated the idea of doing even the simplest spell in public, but she agreed.

Adam grasped her hand, closed his eyes, and whispered a chant:

> *Echo and hum, racket and din,*
> *Clamor and clatter, outside and in*
> *Hush to silence, heed our call*
> *To tacit peace and quiet do fall*

Adam opened his eyes to recite the final line: "*Voices we seek, rise above all.*"

The sensation was similar to the moment just before passing out, or diving under water. Every sound blended into a quiet mumbling hum. Then two distinct voices emerged crystal clear.

Faye asked, "You want me?"

It was just as Cassie had suspected. Beatrix was tempting Faye to join the dark Circle, and Faye was taking the bait.

"Of course." Beatrix's skin shimmered, pale and smooth and new. Her voice was equally smooth but aged with experience.

She focused her flat, level eyes on Faye. "We have a very specific mission for you. We need you to steal the Book of Shadows from Cassandra. Now that Scarlett was stupid enough to let it slip away."

Faye made no immediate response, but she seemed to be mulling this challenge over.

Beatrix continued talking in a low, steady tone. "If only she weren't so pathetic," she said. "You understand what I mean, don't you, Faye? Haven't you always felt deep down that you're smarter than everyone else around you? You'll never reach your full potential in that Circle. They're all cowards but you."

Beatrix was the ancestor who had possessed Faye's body, which meant she was aware of the best way to win Faye to her side. She knew what Faye was unhappy about, and every pet peeve she had with the Circle.

Faye was looking down, faintly nodding.

"Haven't you always felt different, like the black sheep of your own Circle?" Beatrix asked.

Faye's nodding grew less restrained. She met Beatrix's gaze head on, barely able to resist her fixed stare.

"That's exactly how I've felt all my life," Faye said.

"She's weakening by the second," Adam whispered.

"It's because you are different," Beatrix said. "You're much smarter than Scarlett and Cassie."

"So is this a test?" Faye asked. Her voice came out with a tremble. "If I get the book, will I be chosen as your twelfth member?"

Beatrix grinned, and not a single wrinkle appeared around her mouth or eyes. "You've already been chosen. It's up to you now to choose us, and prove your loyalty."

"And then I'll have black magic," Faye said.

"I can't stand to watch this anymore." Adam stood up. "We have to stop her."

Before Cassie could say otherwise, Adam barged in on Faye and Beatrix's conversation, interrupting them mid-sentence.

"Faye, what a surprise to see you," he said, much too loudly.

Faye sat back with a jolt, and Beatrix's expression soured.

"Good thing I ran into you or else you'd be late for school." Adam took Faye by the arm and tried to pull her from her seat. "Come on."

Beatrix stood up briskly, her chair falling back behind her. She took hold of Faye's other arm.

Cassie remained still and straight. "Both of you, let go of her," she said.

Faye was standing up now between Adam and Beatrix, each of them reluctant to release their grip.

Faye eyed Cassie and then wrenched both her wrists free. "I should be going," she said to Beatrix. "I don't want to be late for homeroom."

"We can pick up right where we left off," Beatrix said, completely ignoring Adam's and Cassie's presence. "You know where to find me."

Faye turned on her heel, leaving all three of them standing there, and pushed her way to the door. Cassie and Adam followed after her.

"Hey!" Adam yelled. "We need to talk about what just happened. You have to be stronger than that, Faye. Beatrix had you eating out of her hand."

Faye got to her car and, ignoring Adam, fished through her bag for her keys.

"Faye, we saw you." Adam was still yelling, despite Faye's indifference. "We heard you."

Faye climbed into the front seat of her car and slammed the door closed. She gunned her engine and screeched out of the parking lot.

Adam pursed his lips and looked at Cassie. "She's impossible."

"Maybe we shouldn't jump to conclusions," Cassie said halfheartedly, trying to calm Adam down.

"Are you kidding me? If we hadn't stopped that conversation, how do you think it would have ended up? She would have followed Beatrix's carrot wherever she dangled it, straight to hell."

Cassie knew Adam was right. "We'll keep a closer eye on her," she said. But she knew the real challenge would be keeping Beatrix at bay. And figuring out what key Black John's book contained to destroying the ancestors once and for all.

CHAPTER 19

As Mrs. Walker paced the front of the classroom, giving a lecture on the bubonic plague, Cassie thought about her family. Concentrating became difficult when the brutal historical facts she learned in school could be taken personally. Her ancestors' role in spreading the plague was not an association she was proud of, to say the least. But Mrs. Walker persisted through her lecture nonetheless.

"Circulated by rodents and their fleas," she said, "the bubonic plague, also known as the Black Death, killed an estimated twenty-five million people."

She fiddled with a marker as she walked in figure eights

at the front of the room. "Once bitten," she said, "symp-toms would appear rapidly. Seizures. Delirium. A blacken-ing of the fingers and lips. Vomiting blood and, in some cases, bleeding from the ears."

Cassie cringed. It was a gruesome picture, worsened by the knowledge that the Black Death was actually the Blak Death. *The scientific-minded argued that the plague was spreading through rats*, Timothy had told her. *That was true—but the rats had been bespelled by your ancestors.*

"It was the worst human disaster in history," Mrs. Walker continued. "Society became increasingly violent as more and more people died. Crime was rampant; there was revolt, and persecution."

But what started it all? Cassie had asked Timothy. *What did the Blaks want?*

Timothy's answer had been vague. *Very early on, the man who began your family's Book of Shadows was determined to attain eternal life. He sold his soul, but it backfired. When he died, his bloodline was cursed. And so was his book.*

Mrs. Walker halted her pacing for a moment. "Some people blamed supernatural causes for all the denigra-tion. They'd carve crosses on the front doors of their houses to ward off evil spirits. But we know better today."

Cassie shifted uncomfortably in her chair. She tried to fit the differently shaped pieces of this story together.

"I have a question," she called out as her hand shot up. "How did it all start?"

Mrs. Walker wrinkled her brow at the interruption. "The rats," she said. "Haven't you been listening?"

"But who, and where?" Cassie stuttered. "The origin. Who was the first?"

Mrs. Walker tossed the marker she'd been holding onto her desk. "The first recorded epidemic was as far back as the sixth century, the Byzantine Empire. At the time they called it the Plague of Justinian after the emperor, Justin the first, commonly known as Justinian the Great. The records show he'd been infected, but miraculously survived. His wife succumbed and most of his children, but he lived on for some time, perfectly healthy."

"So he started it?" Cassie said.

Mrs. Walker scowled. "Cassandra, what's gotten into you? You know better. A pandemic can't be blamed on one man." She chuckled condescendingly. "The Plague of Justinian was simply the first outbreak of a disease that would return for generations, in waves. It was most likely brought to the city of Constantinople by infected rodents on grain boats arriving from Egypt. That was the original source of the contagion—not a person."

Cassie tapped her pencil on the surface of her notebook.

Was Justinian the Great the man responsible not only for the Black Death but for her bloodline being cursed?

Was her father's Book of Shadows the book Justinian started?

Was his desire for eternal life still driving him, even now?

A few of the pieces clicked into place in Cassie's mind. But the rest would require an expert.

Cassie tuned back in to the lesson just in time for its conclusion. "It was an age of unprecedented regression," Mrs. Walker pronounced. "A halt on progress that we're not likely to ever see again."

Wishful thinking, Cassie thought. If Faye crossed over and Cassie's assumptions about the ancestors were correct, they would become impervious to destruction. There would be no telling how dark the days ahead would be—forever.

The bell rang, startling Cassie from that final reflection. She dashed for the door, feeling like she was literally racing against time. She had to find Adam and Diana, and they needed to leave immediately, for a quick road trip—to see Timothy Dent. He might be their last hope.

~~~~~~~~~~

Adam, Diana, and Max all grew quiet at the sight of the library's crumbly gray mortar. "We're going inside there?" Adam asked, shifting gears into park.

"That building looks like it's about to tip over," Max said.

Cassie got out of the car, and the others reluctantly followed behind her.

"Are you sure this place isn't abandoned?" Diana asked, struggling over the uneven ground in her thin ballet flats. She held Max's hand for support. "It doesn't look like anyone's here."

"He's here," Cassie said. She pushed open the creaky door, revealing the dimly lit foyer and tall wooden bookcases she remembered from her last visit.

Timothy was standing behind the same tall countertop, but unlike the previous time, his head shot up immediately.

Cassie could tell he'd been expecting her.

"Mr. Dent," she said from across the long hall of stone-gray squares.

"Who is this stranger?" he asked defensively.

"Two members of my Circle," Cassie said. "Adam Conant and Diana Meade."

"No. Him!" Timothy shouted, cutting Cassie off. He was pointing his long, wrinkled finger at Max.

Max held his breath. He backed away toward the door they'd entered through. Cassie understood that Timothy must somehow sense that Max was a witch-hunter.

She reached out and grabbed Max's wrist to keep him from going back to the car.

"He's one of us," she said to Timothy. "He's a former hunter, but he's proven his loyalty to our Circle. Without him, it wouldn't have been possible to get my friends back from the demons."

Timothy eyed Max for a few seconds, then the three of them as a group. "Well, I'm glad to know the exorcism spell worked," he said, letting his guard down for the first time since they'd arrived. "For what reason are you here?"

Cassie stepped forward, and the others followed. Timothy was wearing the same black short-sleeved dress shirt Cassie had last seen him in. Again, it was streaked with dust. *Does he ever wash his clothes?* she wondered.

"We need your help," Cassie said.

Timothy scoffed. "I figured that much."

"I was able to perform the exorcism," Cassie replied. "But the ancestor spirits returned to their corporeal form. Now they're free in New Salem and trying to secure a twelfth member to bind their Circle."

Timothy's gray eyes went still, but they revealed no surprise. He turned toward his office.

Cassie assumed they were expected to follow him. The four of them entered the double glass doors in a straight line and found places to sit down.

Timothy scrambled through a number of cabinets and file drawers, stacking a few books and folders upon his desk before falling into his brown leather chair.

"As I feared, Absolom must have altered the exorcism," he said. "He recrafted it to a resurrection."

"So we did exactly what he wanted us to do," Adam said.

Timothy gave a nod to Cassie. "She did, yes."

"I did what *you* told me to!" Cassie shot back.

Timothy squinted his eyes and squeezed the bridge of his nose. "Please, no shouting. Your voice goes right through me."

"Why didn't you tell me about Justinian the Great?" Cassie said.

Timothy's eyes opened wide. His mouth fanned to a

crooked, toothy smile. "You've been doing your home-
work. Good for you."

"He was the man who began my family's Book of
Shadows," Cassie said. "The one you told me was determined to attain eternal life."

"Yes, I told you he sold his soul," Timothy said. "I told
you when he died, his bloodline and his book were cursed."

"You didn't tell me his name," Cassie said. "Why?"

"His name doesn't matter."

"Why wouldn't it matter?" Cassie persisted.

Timothy's face reddened.

"You can't only tell me half the story," Cassie said.
"You're either willing to help us or you're not. If your
hatred for my father is what's preventing you from—"

"His name changed!" Timothy shouted.

Cassie was startled by his anger. They all were.

Timothy pointed to a portrait on the wall behind his
desk. "Justinian the first," he said. "He's the source. Are
you happy?"

Cassie gazed at the crowned man, decorated in the
riches of an emperor. A circle enclosed his head like a
saint's halo.

"He was determined to attain eternal life," Timothy
said. "But he still died. And when he managed to rise from

the dead, he died again. And the final time he resurrected himself, you and your Circle killed him."

Cassie's heart went still. "Do you mean—"

Timothy brushed down his few white hairs that flared up during his brief rage. "Your father was the source, Cassie," he said more calmly. "But all your ancestors have left of him is that book. His drive for eternal life lives on in them. It's their quest now."

Cassie allowed herself a few seconds to think, to adjust. She could see the shock of her own face reflected on the faces of her friends. "Does my mother know?" she asked.

Timothy shook his head. "Not even your grandmother knew. It's taken me my whole life to figure it out."

"It makes sense," Cassie said. "The way the book clings to me."

"Mr. Dent," Diana said, "Cassie overheard the ancestors talking about a spell." But before she could say anything more, Timothy cut her off.

"It's an eternal-life spell. That's what the ancestors have come back for. But lucky for you they need a bound Circle, and it has to be done beneath a full moon."

"Yeah, lucky," Max said sarcastically.

Cassie took one last look at the awful painting of

Justinian I. "So what do we do now?" she asked. "Can they be stopped?"

"I'm not sure," Timothy said. "I was on the trail of figuring out this spell when I was stripped of my powers sixteen years ago."

He leaned in uncomfortably close to Cassie. "When *your father* stripped me of my powers sixteen years ago."

His breath smelled of fried onions.

"If you can manage to burn Black John's book using this spell," he continued, mercifully backing away, "it will destroy the book's dark magic and the demons that came out of it. Including the demon that originated in Justinian the Great."

Timothy unrolled a parchment scroll upon his desk and weighted it down to keep it from flapping closed. It contained the tiny, carefully handwritten text of his spell.

"The ancestor spirits are bonded to the book just like you are, Cassie," Timothy said. "But for them, it's their life force."

Cassie scrutinized the scroll's painstaking text.

Adam grabbed a magnifying glass from Timothy's desk and honed in on a few specifics. "If the Circle uses this spell to burn the book before the eternal-life spell happens," Adam asked, "we'll be free from these demons forever?"

Timothy closed one eye and nodded. "If you do it right, all the dark magic that grew out of the book will be eliminated."

He waddled back around his desk, mumbling. "I was robbed of my power just before I had the chance to perform this spell, and no one else would try it. They were too wary of the consequences. And not a single one of them would lend me their power, either. Not a single witch in all of New Salem."

"I get the sense you're still not telling us the whole story," Diana said. "Why wouldn't anyone try the spell? What consequences were they afraid of?"

Timothy's eyes flared at Diana's forwardness.

Cassie shot her a look to be quiet. The last thing they needed was for Timothy to kick them out now.

"All magic has consequences," he said curtly. "It's the simple law of cause and effect."

"Of course," Adam said. "We understand that." He picked up the parchment scroll and began rolling it back into its container. "This is exactly what we need."

"You need more than just that, young man." Timothy pulled a set of dull metal keys from his desk drawer and shuffled over to an iron cabinet within the wall that resembled a bank vault. He unlocked it, opened the enormous door, and disappeared for a moment inside.

He reappeared carrying a large wooden box. "You must burn Black John's book," he said. "But you need a complete Circle to do it. You will also need everything in here."

He handed the box to Max. "It's heavier than it looks," he said. "But you have big muscles."

Max half-smiled, unsure what to do with the box for a moment, before deciding to set it down on his chair.

It was sealed tightly shut with tarnished brass latch closures, but it didn't appear to be locked.

"Go on, open it," Timothy said.

Max lifted the top off the box and began digging through it. It was filled with neatly folded ceremonial robes, crystals, incense, and candles.

As Cassie, Diana, and Adam examined its contents, Timothy disappeared into the vault again. He returned carrying a similar, smaller wooden box that he handed to Cassie.

Cassie set the box down upon Timothy's desk and reached for both latches.

"No, not now," Timothy said urgently. "Don't open

this one until you have no other choice. It's the only way."

Cassie looked at Adam, then Diana and Max. "But what's inside?" she asked Timothy.

"I hope you can do what I failed to years ago," Timothy said. He either didn't hear her question or simply chose to ignore it.

Cassie had a bad feeling about this.

CHAPTER 20

Cassie stood surrounded by the faces of her friends as Coach Kaelin's whistle echoed from the football field. It was the next day at school, and the Circle was having a meeting under the bleachers. Max was among them. He and Diana sat side by side on the ground, fiddling with each other's fingers, unable to suppress smiles in spite of the dire circumstances. If only the Circle could induct Max as their twelfth member, Cassie thought. A hunter initiation, imagine that.

Adam looked up at Cassie, waiting for her to break the news of what they'd learned from Timothy to the rest of the group. He'd barely taken his eyes off her since they'd left Concord, understanding without her having to tell him that this new revelation about her father's history was weighing on her. Would she never truly be rid of him? But as Timothy said, it was the ancestors who were the Circle's problem—they were the ones on the brink of attaining immortality, closer than Cassie's father had ever gotten, in all his wretched lifetimes.

Nick had on a dark pair of sunglasses so Cassie couldn't see his eyes, but she could feel that he was looking at her. She pretended not to notice. Truth be told, she'd been avoiding him as she and Adam were becoming more and more inseparable. It wasn't the most mature way of dealing with her conflicted feelings, but for now it was the best she could do.

"We've learned that the ancestors are after more than just revenge," Cassie said to the group.

"Who's 'we'?" Faye called out.

"A few of us went to see a man my mother told me about," Cassie replied. "He's devoted his life to studying my family. And he told us that the ancestors' plan is to perform an eternal-life spell. That's why they need a twelfth member."

She passed her eyes over each of them. Cassie had all the faith in the world in her Circle, but these dark ancestors had a lot to offer. Limitless power. Everlasting life. And after losing so many loved ones to the hunters recently, she wouldn't blame anyone for being tempted.

"But if we secure a twelfth member before they do," Cassie said, "and perform a spell to burn my father's book, the ancestors will be destroyed forever."

"No sweat," Doug said mockingly.

Nick turned away for a moment and slid his sunglasses down. "Do you hear that?"

Cassie listened. There was a whistling coming from the trees. "The wind?" she asked. And then her ears popped as if free-falling on a roller coaster.

The whole Circle flinched, jerking their necks back. It was a shared sensation, whatever was happening.

Cassie's vision hazed; the surrounding world went fuzzy.

"I can't see," Sean said. "What's going on?"

An image appeared before Cassie's eyes, as if in a dream. It was a room, an elaborate ballroom, with marble pillars and a gilded gold ceiling. It was crowded with people dressed in fancy clothes, dancing and laughing, drinking champagne from long-stemmed glass flutes. Cassie was overcome with a sense of well-being, by the gentle energy of their rich joviality—until the shock of a shattering glass broke the scene. Everyone began to scream. The lights flickered, and the edges of the image darkened, like an aging photograph. No, Cassie realized—like a photograph burning slowly over a flame. The ornate ballroom, the revelatory guests, the once strong pillars, crumpled and blackened until they disappeared to ash.

Then came a voice. Absolom's booming tongue. "Tonight," he said, "New Salem burns."

Cassie snapped awake. Her ears popped a second time, and her vision cleared.

Nick came into view, looking around with his sunglasses suspended in his fingers. Adam and Diana blinked, adjusting their eyes.

"I guess this means we're going to the benefit tonight," Faye said.

"Is that what that place was?" Doug asked.

Melanie nodded. "The New Salem Historical Society benefit. The ancestors are going to burn it to the ground."

So this was the great revenge the ancestors had been building up to. Cassie realized it made perfect sense. The benefit was the ideal place to take vengeance on New Salem. Everyone who was anyone would be there.

"Why would they give us this warning?" Chris asked.

"Because they don't want us to miss it," Deborah said.

Nick finally put his sunglasses back on. "We have to try to stop them."

"How?" Melanie said, almost to herself. "They're so much more powerful than us. The only way we can stop them is to destroy them."

"Melanie's right," Diana said. "All the more reason we need to complete our Circle. Our only hope is to get Scarlett to cross over."

"Like that'll ever happen," Faye murmured. "Stopping the ancestors from destroying the benefit is one thing. Getting Scarlett to come to our side is another."

Cassie thought back to Scarlett's initiation. After the hunters killed Suzan and Scarlett inherited her place in the Circle, it had felt like the worst thing in the world. If only Cassie had known then just how incorrect that premonition was. Things had since gotten *much* worse.

"How could we possibly win Scarlett over?" Laurel's voice cracked with frustration. "What do we have to tempt her with? Nothing that competes with being all-powerful and having eternal life."

Cassie studied Adam's face. He was looking down, seemingly lost in his own thoughts, totally unprepared for what Cassie was about to bring to the table.

"We have Adam," Cassie said, and his head shot up.

"Scarlett wants Adam," she said declaratively. "He's our best shot to win her over."

Adam stuttered, unable to find the right words. He shook his head. "No." Slowly, painfully, he said, "That can't be our only option."

A cold determination flooded Cassie's veins. "There's no escaping this," she said.

Diana placed a comforting hand on Cassie's shoulder. "That's a brave sacrifice to make."

At first Cassie thought Diana meant it was a brave sacrifice for Adam to make, then she realized that Diana was speaking to her.

Only after Cassie acknowledged Diana's compliment did she turn her attention to Adam. "You have to do it," Diana said to him. "For the Circle."

Adam stared straight down at the ground as if he couldn't face any of them. "How do I . . ." He paused.

Faye laughed out loud. "I think you know exactly how, Adam. You already have."

Adam looked sadly at Cassie, and she strained to return his gaze with love. She had to be calm now. She couldn't lose control.

Bleary-eyed and nauseated, she said, "You have to use the benefit to get closer to Scarlett. Convince her you're in love with her, not me. It's our only hope of getting her to cross over."

"We'll all be there with you," Diana added.

"You can't say no, man," Nick said.

"Alright," Adam said finally. "I'll do it for the Circle."

And though it's what Cassie had insisted upon, something inside her shattered.

-----

*Sally Waltman was the flyer on New Salem High's cheer-*leading squad. Cassie watched from the bleachers as she got tossed, flipped, and thrown about, all while maintaining her bright white smile. *Sally is really something,* Cassie thought, *an overachiever in the best way.* And she came from a long line of prominence. Her father was the chairman of the board of the Historical Society—that's why Cassie had come to watch her practice. It was time to take Sally up on her offer to help the Circle.

Sally had spotted Cassie midway through practice, so when the squad broke up, she headed straight in her direction. Her face was flushed and shiny, and she dabbed it softly with a white towel. "What's up?"

"I need a favor," Cassie said. "But that's not the worst of it."

Sally flipped her towel back in a roll around her tiny

shoulders and took a seat beside Cassie. "Don't leave any-thing out."

Cassie described how the ancestors planned to trap everyone inside the Historical Society benefit and then burn the place to the ground.

Sally kept her eyes on her teammates making their way across the field to the locker room. "After what they did to the auditorium, I doubt they're bluffing."

She seemed to be replaying the horror of that event in her mind, frame by frame, the color leaching from her face. "I can't tell my dad. Not without explaining how I know."

"You shouldn't," Cassie said. "The Circle will stop them, but we need to be there. Can you get us in?"

"That's a given; I'll put you all on the list. But how will you stop them, Cassie? All the people who'll be at that benefit . . . I can't imagine . . ."

"We'll do whatever we can," Cassie said, careful not to make any false promises. "Armed with defense spells, we'll counter them one for one, the way Nick and I managed to do at the auditorium."

It almost sounded like a plan. But what Cassie didn't mention was that in the auditorium she was battling her possessed friends. The ancestors were much stronger and more powerful now that they had their own bodies.

Sally brushed back a strand of hair that had fallen in front of her eye, and Cassie noticed her hand tremble.

"I won't let anyone get hurt," Cassie said. "You have nothing to worry about."

It was the false promise she probably shouldn't make, but it seemed to calm Sally. She rose and stepped down the bleachers toward the field.

"I'll see you there," she said.

～～～～～～～～～～

*Cassie unzipped the garment bag holding her beaded halter-*neck evening dress. Diana crossed her bedroom to admire it.

"It's beautiful," she said. "Is it new?"

"Suzan picked it out for me, one day when we were shopping," Cassie said. "I told her I had no use for an evening dress, but she insisted I buy it. She said it was too perfect to pass up."

Faye looked away, and all the girls got quiet.

Suzan had always been the best when it came to prepping for a fancy party, so it was with a little bit of a heavy heart that Cassie and the others continued the tradition in her absence.

"I've been thinking about her all night," Deborah said.

Laurel marveled at the dress's intricate beadwork. "We all are," she said.

Now it was Diana's bedroom instead of Suzan's serving as the backdrop to their primping. It looked like a movie studio dressing room. There were backlit mirrors propped up on every flat surface, curlers warming on the dresser, perfume in the air.

Melanie directed Cassie to sit down on the chair facing the largest mirror. "We've got to get your hair done," she said. "What are you feeling tonight, up or down?"

"Do it up," Laurel shouted from inside Diana's closet.

Cassie agreed. "Up," she said, and Melanie went to work, massaging lavender-scented oil onto her scalp.

Cassie closed her eyes, enjoying the soothing smell of the oil and Melanie's strong fingers kneading the tension from her temples. For a moment everything felt like normal. What a long-missed luxury it was to listen to her friends debate over something as insignificant as which dress most brought out the color of their eyes, and which shoes made them appear taller but not too much taller.

Faye stepped out of the bathroom holding up two nearly identical skimpy black satin dresses. "I can't decide," she said to Deborah. "Which one?"

Deborah, who was lounging on Diana's bed already

dressed in a white tuxedo with purple trim, somehow noticed a distinction between the dresses. "That one," she said definitively, pointing to the one on the left.

"That's what I thought, too," Faye said.

Diana asked Cassie to zip up her pearl-colored gown. It cascaded down her legs in a long, flowing train.

Cassie caught herself relaxing. She almost felt happy. But then Diana began talking about Max.

"This'll be our first fancy party as a couple," she said, and that was all it took for the girl talk to veer into the territory of boys.

Cassie grew sullen and quiet. She remembered the stomach-curdling fact she'd been striving to force away— that Adam would be spending the night flirting with Scarlett.

"Cassie," Diana said, "come back to us."

Cassie tried to smile.

"You have nothing to worry about," Laurel said. "Whatever happened with Scarlett while Adam was possessed only happened because he was possessed. He was literally someone else."

"You'd have to be possessed to get with that girl," Deborah added.

"Adam couldn't stray from you even if he wanted to,"

Melanie said into the mirror, with a bobby pin between her lips. "That cord works better than a short leash."

Cassie exchanged a nervous glance with Diana that gave all the girls pause.

"What was that?" Faye asked, stepping between them. "One of those words made you uncomfortable, either *cord* or *leash*, and either way we want to hear the story."

Diana averted her eyes, but Cassie said Faye was right. She turned around on her chair to face them and described the cord that had appeared between Adam and Scarlett.

"The first time I saw it was when I was half-unconscious after battling Scarlett at the broken-down cottage on Hawthorne Street," Cassie said. "And the second time, it caught Adam off guard the night of the spring dance."

"How is that even possible?" Melanie asked.

"I don't understand how," Cassie said. "I wish it wasn't real, but it is."

Diana's lips formed a pout. Even she was at a loss for what to say to make the truth less painful.

Melanie was mentally sorting through this new information. "So when Adam was possessed," she said, "and he and Scarlett were so close . . ."

"It wasn't just the possession making him act crazy like

we thought," Laurel said. "He and Scarlett have an actual connection?"

Cassie's heart sank. "I guess it's possible to have more than one soul mate. At least if you're Adam."

Melanie and Laurel stared down at the carpet, heartbroken for Cassie.

Then Deborah hopped off Diana's bed. She placed one hand on Faye's shoulder and the other on Cassie's.

"I don't know about the rest of you," she said. "But I will personally take Scarlett out with a debeautifying spell tonight if she tries anything with Adam."

Faye gave Deborah a high five. "Now you're talking! We'll make her so ugly that the sight of her will make babies cry."

Cassie let herself laugh. It was going to be a difficult night, but she was glad she had her friends back on her side.

CHAPTER 21

The town hall ballroom, with its marble floors and high ceil-
ings, was the setting for all formal events in New Salem—
and the Historical Society benefit was the nicest event of
all. Tonight's party would be crowded with the town's elite:
academics, politicians, and everyone wealthy enough to
spring for a table.

Cassie spotted Sally across the dance floor, dressed in a
peach cocktail dress with a bow around the waist. She was
standing with Max.

"They're already here," Sally said, pointing to Scarlett
and the group of ancestors huddled in the corner.

They appeared more sinister than ever in formal wear.

Absolom, whose dark hair was slicked back with a shiny gel, murmured something while looking at Cassie, and the group exploded with laughter.

"No sign of Adam yet?" Diana asked, extending her hand to Max. He wore a gray suit that was just tight enough to show off his physique.

Melanie scanned the crowd. "Nope."

Laurel glanced at the corners of the room and each emergency exit. "There's nothing out of the ordinary going on," she said. "Yet."

Faye gave Deborah a nudge. "Let's go get a drink."

Cassie checked the door at the exact moment Nick stepped inside. He was wearing a black suit and tie, and for once he had traded his leather boots for a pair of shiny oxfords.

He headed straight for Cassie. "I hear you came here stag," he said playfully. "Does that mean I get the first dance?"

Melanie raised her eyebrows and politely led Laurel away. Diana was off somewhere with Max.

Cassie allowed herself to smile. "If we can stop whatever's coming tonight, I'll dance straight through till morning."

"Is that a promise?" Nick said. "Because I'll hold you to it."

Sean, Chris, and Doug entered the doorway and caught sight of Nick and Cassie immediately. They made their way over, almost unrecognizably clean-cut in tailored suits and their hair combed back.

"Any action yet?" Chris asked.

Cassie gazed around the enormous room. The black-and-white tiled floor reminded her of dance scenes in old classic movies. It gave way to marble pillars and cloth-covered banquet tables. Since this was a benefit for the Historical Society, the walls and tables were adorned with New Salem history pieces on loan from the museum—statues of prominent figures, old maps in glass frames, photographs of the founding families.

The ancestors eyed it all like vultures preparing for a feast. Sally's father was too busy shaking hands and smiling for cameras to notice. He and his board members had not a clue what was coming. Equally oblivious, the Outsiders drifted around them, enjoying appetizers off silver trays. *Lambs to a slaughter*, Cassie thought.

Cassie noticed Alice and Beatrix had broken off from the others. They whispered to one another, conspiring, in the corner.

Alice's dress was black, long, and straight. It could have been very old, or just designed to look that way. Beatrix's was similar, but she wore a red shawl over her shoulders.

Cassie approached them.

"So, you made it," Alice said in her deep monotone.

"I told you they wouldn't miss it," Beatrix said.

Alice set her heartbreaking eyes on Cassie. "We're going to seal this place like a tomb," she said. "Then the fire will rage. Do you know what it feels like to be burned alive, Cassie?"

"I do," Beatrix said. "The skin of your face melts first. Then your neck. Your hands, as if they could protect you from the relentless flames. You'll be wide awake, more awake than you've ever been, and you can smell yourself cooking. Flesh bakes so slowly, Cassie. It seems to take forever."

Cassie cringed. "No one here tonight is burning alive," she said. "My Circle won't allow it."

Just then Adam appeared in the doorway, wearing his best blue-gray suit. He offered Cassie a quick apologetic glance as he headed toward Nick, Chris, and Doug, who were sloppily progressing through an hors d'oeuvre plate of sliders.

While he ate and laughed with the guys, Adam eyed Scarlett and the ancestors gathered in the back corner. Within a few minutes he casually got himself a drink and meandered toward them.

Feeling Alice's and Beatrix's eyes on her, Cassie did her best to look distressed by the idea of Adam going over to talk to Scarlett. It wasn't hard to do as she made out the thin cord drawing them together.

Cassie watched Adam closely. His face had relaxed in Scarlett's presence.

"Look at that smile," Beatrix said, nodding toward Adam. "You can't fake a smile that bright. It's obvious he's smitten."

Adam led Scarlett onto the dance floor. Cassie tried to remind herself that he was playing a part, but his affection seemed so real.

Scarlett ran her fingers up and down the length of his suit-jacketed arm. Did he shudder? No, it was more of a quiver.

Adam's flirting had to be convincing. It was the Circle's only hope of getting Scarlett on their side. But within a few minutes of watching them, everyone else in the room dropped away, and Cassie began to sweat.

Scarlett had secured Adam's rapt attention. She was speaking softly to him, her face up close to his, swaying to the music. And he was leaning in slightly, watching her mouth, those full red lips of hers getting perilously close to his own.

But when Scarlett went in for a kiss, Adam quickly backed away. That was where he drew the line. Scarlett had leaned in and kissed the air.

Cassie took a breath. Her tunnel vision ceased, the room came back to life, and all the other guests reappeared.

Adam, when he was really Adam, couldn't betray her.

"You should seriously reconsider your previous decision to snub us, Cassandra," Beatrix said. "Look around."

She directed Cassie's gaze around the room. "All of these innocent people are about to die."

Alice placed her cold, bony hand on Cassie's shoulder. "Wouldn't you rather be on our side than theirs?"

"No," Cassie said firmly. She shook herself from Alice's grip.

"Our side is going to win." Alice's eyes were smoldering, but Cassie wouldn't be intimidated.

"No!" she screamed out again, not caring who heard her over the jazz band.

Alice let out an exasperated breath and turned away. "Forget this," she said to Beatrix. "Let's bring this place down."

Wasting no more time, Alice signaled to Absolom, ordering the ancestors into action.

Before Cassie could even raise a hand in protest, the centerpiece of the ballroom, a stone statue of New Salem's first mayor, exploded to a million bits that scattered across the checkered floor like hardened raindrops.

People screamed and ducked, covering their heads. Cassie's friends searched for one another through the pandemonium.

Mr. Waltman, Sally's father, waved his arms. "Just a freak accident," he called out. "Nobody panic. Is everyone okay?"

Then another statue burst, and another. The black-and-white floor rumbled. Plaques slid down the walls. Mr. Waltman covered his balding head and began running, along with the rest of the crowd, toward the exit.

"Earthquake!" people yelled.

Cassie and her friends had anticipated this. They huddled close to each other and bound their energy.

"Power of Earth," Diana said, leading the defense spell. "We call upon you to protect us, to help us defend this room and the innocent people in it from harm."

A momentary calm swept through the air, enough to trick the terrified Outsiders into believing the worst had passed.

But the ancestors countered the Circle's defense with

an even stronger attack, breaking down their protective barrier.

All the smashed stone and shattered glass upon the floor whirled into the air like a tornado. It spun through the room, a storm gone wild, destroying everything in its wake.

A ruined brass picture frame boomeranged toward the back of Sally's head. Max dove, knocking her out of harm's way just in time.

The Circle cast another spell. This time Cassie took the lead. "Guardians of the defenseless," she called. "We entreat you! Combatants of right causes, join us against this malevolent attack. Let the innocent rise up against this evil."

But the ancestors were too powerful. A dark shadow descended upon the room, like night. The Outsiders banged on every exit door to no avail. There was no way out. They were sealed in, just like Alice had said.

Smoke clouded the air. Max and Sally tried breaking down one of the doors, using a table as a battering ram, while the Circle's defense spells continued to falter.

Cassie exchanged a look with Adam. He had joined the Circle in their attempts to block the ancestors' destruction, forgetting his feigned allegiance to Scarlett.

"They're so strong," he said. "You have to do something, Cassie. You're the only one."

Deep down Cassie had known it would come to this. Her black magic was their solitary chance. She went inward to her darkest place and stirred around for the right words. A heat flooded her veins just as the ballroom caught fire.

Cassie felt her eyes harden like calluses. She raised her arms and stretched her fingers taut.

> *Malignis vis intra me, perdere hoc malum.*
> *Purgare eam. Purgare.*
> *Haec entia non gerunt nequam auctoritas!*

Cassie's whole body trembled. The flames crawling up the ballroom walls settled, as if in sudden fear.

Absolom shouted out new instructions in a language Cassie couldn't understand. The ancestors lifted their hands, and the fire roared twice as high as before.

It was at that moment that Cassie realized the Circle was going to lose. All along the ancestors had been holding back, merely toying with them—with her.

This was their show.

Outsiders began collapsing left and right from smoke

inhalation. Many fell unconscious. Max and Sally lay on the ground among them. Those who were still awake were hysterical, tumbling over one another. They shrieked and cried for help, banging senselessly on the locked doors. It sounded to Cassie like hell on earth.

She wanted to run, but she couldn't. Yet she couldn't fight either. She had nothing left. This room would be their shared, ovenlike tomb. Hers and her Circle's, and the town's. It was over, at last.

Then Absolom clapped his hands three times, and the room fell silent. All movement ceased. Only the ancestors and the Circle remained cognizant.

"You've already lost," Alice said. "But we're willing to make you an offer."

Cassie exchanged a cautious look with Adam.

"These people can still go home tonight, safely," Alice said. "If one of you is willing to cross over right now."

"These Outsiders won't remember a thing," Beatrix added. "It's in your hands."

Cassie turned to her friends. They were exhausted, defeated. All the historical relics had been destroyed, reduced to charcoal and ash.

It *wasn't* in their hands, Cassie thought. Because suffering would still be the end result, it was only a question of when. Either way, she'd failed to protect New Salem as she'd promised Sally she would—as she'd promised herself she would.

"I'll do it!" Faye shouted out.

Cassie felt a writhe of panic in her stomach.

"Call off the fire," Faye said to the ancestors. "And I'm yours."

With a nod from Absolom, Alice waved her hand and the flames died, the smoke dissipated.

"Come," Alice said.

Faye stepped across the black-and-white ballroom floor with a confident stride.

Alice rested her heartbroken eyes on Cassie while Samuel, Charlotte, and Thomas gathered around Faye, drawing her in, murmuring their approval.

"We should do something," Nick said.

Melanie agreed. "We can't let this happen."

But no one made a move to cut in. There was really nothing to be done. The Circle, and Cassie alone, had expended all of their energy, and it wasn't nearly enough.

"Faye's only going with them to save all these people," Deborah whispered. "She's doing the right thing."

Diana looked to Cassie. "But we can't just let them have her, right?"

Beatrix wrapped her arm around Faye.

"You were my first choice all along," she said, leading her to the door. She opened it with a silent spell. "Let's go home."

~~~~~~~~~~~~~~

Adam rushed to catch up with Cassie as she made a beeline for the door, trying to get away before anyone could see her cry. It was all just too much. At a certain point a girl had to break.

Adam caught her by the wrist. "Can I at least walk you home?" he asked.

Cassie agreed, but as they trudged down the road neither of them said much. Cassie watched the ground, feeling silly now in her fancy clothes and makeup in the midst of so much defeat.

"It's going to be okay," Adam said. "We'll figure out how to get Faye back."

He put his arm around Cassie's bare shoulders.

"I'm not so sure," Cassie said. "Defeating the ancestors feels so impossible."

Adam came to a standstill and made Cassie face him. His hands trembled slightly on her arms.

"This is not over yet. And you're not giving up," he said. "I won't let you."

It amazed Cassie how Adam never lost his hope, how he never surrendered to defeat or despair. He truly was one of a kind.

"And did I mention how beautiful you look tonight?" he added.

"Well," Cassie said, "in spite of the great failure of the night, at least you aren't going home with Scarlett."

"Were you worried about that?" he asked, sounding honestly surprised. "I only did all of that because you told me to."

"I wasn't worried," Cassie lied. She rested her head on Adam's chest and breathed him in. "But I'll take whatever small victory I can get right now."

Then she lifted her head and kissed him softly on the lips.

CHAPTER 22

Gathered in the secret room, everyone's body language spoke for them. Melanie, Laurel, and Deborah hunched in their chairs. Diana and Max slumped on the bed. The guys were sprawled across the sofa, slouching as if holding up their own heads took too much effort. The words no one said aloud were that the next full moon was only three nights away. It wasn't much time before the ancestors would be a threat forever.

Cassie disappeared to the kitchen and returned with some snacks to liven the mood. She set down a plate of cookies and a bowl of popcorn that nobody touched, and then sat beside Adam on the couch.

Deborah took the floor. "Our magic isn't strong enough against them," she said. "How are we supposed to rescue Faye?"

Sean widened his eyes. "We should burn down the warehouse."

Chris approved, but Doug shook his head. "That'll never work."

"We only need to distract the ancestors long enough to give Faye a chance to escape," Diana said. "Maybe a fire would do the trick."

"I have a better idea." Laurel stood up. *"Somnus pulvis,"* she said, looking at Diana. "Sleep powder."

"Seriously?" Chris laughed out loud. "You think a little pixie dust can take down the most powerful witches of all time?"

"For about two or three minutes," Laurel said defensively. "And that's all we need to get Faye out of there."

She turned to Cassie. "I was up all night studying the ingredients. All we have to do is get it into their eyes and they'll go right down."

Cassie tried to sound appreciative. "That sounds great, Laurel, but I don't think any potion or powder will work on a demon."

"A regular potion won't," Laurel said. "But if I spell it, and mix in the proper herbs, it will."

Diana's face broke into a half-smile. It was the first of its kind all day. "You really think you can do it?"

"Of course she can," Melanie said. "Laurel's a genius!"

Laurel pulled a slip of paper out of her pocket and began reading off ingredients. "We'll need lavender, chamomile, valerian, boneset, foxglove, marjoram."

"What are we waiting for?" Adam stood up. "Let's head to the garden."

Cassie followed the group outside. It was a long shot, one she wasn't even sure she believed would work. But seeing her Circle hopeful was worth going along with the idea.

———————

*As soon as it grew dark outside, the Circle left for the ware-*house. They'd collected all the ingredients from Laurel's list, crushed them into a fine powder, and spelled it with magic. They each held a small felt sack of that powder now, to be tossed into the eyes of their enemies.

Their plan of action was straightforward: stun the ancestors, put them to sleep, rescue Faye. Every Circle member had an ancestor to target. Cassie would pursue Scarlett.

Nick checked the loose pane in the warehouse's back window. "These ancestors are so cocky," he whispered, "they still haven't bothered to cast a guarding spell to keep us out."

They hadn't even secured the broken window, Cassie realized. They obviously revered themselves as too powerful to take such precautions.

Nick pulled aside the loose pane, and the Circle climbed through, catlike, one at a time. The ancestors didn't hear them come in. They were seated in the main room having a discussion, totally unguarded. Cassie squeezed her fistful of powder in her right hand and located Scarlett leaning on a crate, off to the side of the group.

"Let's go," Nick said, and the Circle descended upon them, scattering into battle.

Adam was the first to hurl his fistful of dust into Absolom's eyes.

Absolom blinked rapidly and hobbled on his feet for a few seconds, then covered his face and screamed. He fell over onto the floor as an acidic smell rose to the air. His skin sizzled gruesomely beneath his hands. Cassie wasn't sure what was happening.

Laurel was horrified, but she still managed to hurl her dust into Charlotte's face.

Diana took out Alice. Deborah handled Beatrix. It may as well have been battery acid they were throwing, singeing the ancestors' eyes and faces so badly that an acrid cloud of smoke filled the room. They dropped, shrieking, one by one.

Cassie locked eyes with Faye, standing with her hands down at her sides in the middle of all the action. She didn't move; she appeared mesmerized that this battle was being fought on her behalf—that she was the prize.

Scarlett raised her hands in defense, to stop Cassie's approach with a spell, but it only took one second to heave her handful of toxic dust into Scarlett's eyes. She went down, the same as the others, writhing on the floor between Samuel and Thomas.

Soon Faye was the last left standing. The Circle assembled around her.

"Come on, Faye," Cassie said. "Let's get you out of here."

"Quickly," Melanie added. "We may only have a few minutes."

Faye began backing away. "What makes you so sure I want to leave?"

The ancestors were already climbing up to their feet, but they still cradled their faces and covered their burning eyes.

"Faye," Diana said, reaching out to her, but Faye batted Diana away. "No," she said. "I like it here. They understand me. And they have power, real power."

"We don't have time for this!" Melanie shouted.

"I'm not coming with you," Faye said.

Deborah grabbed her by the arms. "Yes, you are." She tried to wrestle Faye toward the window, but Faye pushed her off, filled with rage. She splayed her fingernails, which were long and painted bloodred.

"I've learned a few new spells since I've been here," she threatened. "Don't make me show you."

Cassie centered her energy. Faye left her with no choice but to use magic against her. A simple binding spell would do. Just enough to haul Faye out of here.

But before Cassie could get the words out, Laurel screamed.

Absolom was firmly on his feet. He let out a muffled groan and shook his head from side to side. His eyes were singed, the skin around them pink and raw, but he could see.

Cassie shot Faye with her spell, but Faye blocked it with a deflection.

Then Alice lurched forward.

"Retreat!" Diana yelled out.

Faye still had her hands set and ready to defend herself against any spell hurled her way.

Cassie gave Diana a nod. "Retreat," she repeated, and everyone fled to the open window.

Cassie was the last to jump through. By the time the fresh air hit her face, she heard all the ancestors grumbling, swearing their revenge. The smell of their scalded flesh was still strong in the air.

Cassie ran with the others toward Chris's rusted Jeep. Sean gripped the leather steering wheel, ready to gun the accelerator as Cassie climbed into the back. In all, the Circle was a sorry sight.

Melanie patted Laurel on the back. "I know the powder didn't do what we thought, but it still did the job."

Gentle Laurel was too traumatized by her potion's grotesque effectiveness to reply.

"I hadn't expected Faye to put up that much of a fight," Deborah said, breathing heavily.

"I guess we took for granted that she only crossed over to save the people at the benefit," Diana said. "So much for that idea."

Cassie said nothing. What was there to say? The clock was ticking, and their chances of winning back Faye's loyalty weren't looking good, not good at all.

It was the middle of the night when Cassie sprang awake. She'd been thinking about Faye in her sleep, replaying the scenes of her crossing over and the Circle's failed attempt at winning her back, in different combinations. In each version the details changed, but the outcome always remained the same: failure. Coming up short.

There was no use trying to go back to sleep now. Cassie was too wound up. It felt like two tennis balls had been lodged into the space between her neck and shoulders. She climbed out of bed, wrestled into her favorite hoodie, pulled on her sneakers, and quietly made her way outside.

Unlike Cassie, Crowhaven Road was sound asleep. She could almost hear the street itself snoring peacefully, unconscious to the horror of waking life.

She turned east toward the water, following the smell of salt in the air, to the rocks that guarded the beach. Climbing them strained her muscles, but once she jumped down to the other side of their divide, a stretch of white sand welcomed her. This late at night the beach was deserted, a forsaken paradise. It was quiet enough to hear the waves lapping uninterrupted at the shore.

Cassie looked up at the yellow moon. Only two more

nights till it would be a full bright circle and the ancestors would cast the eternal-life spell.

She inched closer to the water. Out of the corner of her eye she thought she saw a shadow. She searched left, then right. It must have just been her imagination. Then there it was again—for sure this time—a quick, sharp movement behind an outcropping of rock near the water.

Cassie told herself to turn around and run right home, but her legs remained in place like two wooden posts stuck in the sand. Her eyes widened to searchlights. She wanted this, didn't she? Isn't this what she'd come looking for? To just have it out and be done with it already, to end this battle of wills against Scarlett and the ancestors once and for all.

But in the next moment, the shadow detached itself from the rocks and came into view. It wasn't an ancestor or Scarlett. It was Nick.

Cassie felt a jolt at the sight of his face, the rough shape of his shoulders. "You scared me," she said.

Nick stood tall and watched Cassie with steady eyes. "You don't look very scared," he said.

It was true. Her adrenaline was pumping and her heart was fluttering within her chest, but she wasn't afraid. She was excited.

"Cassie," Nick said. He surprised her by taking hold of her arms, just above the elbow. His hands felt strong, rugged, as he squeezed tighter. He grazed his lips against her ear. "I miss you."

If the ancestors had won, Cassie thought, and she really was facing the end of her days, then why not?

Nick's lips found the soft spot on her neck, just below her ear.

If she was soon to die . . .

No.

If she was soon to die, she wanted to die beside Adam. No one else.

"I've been meaning to talk to you, Nick," Cassie said, taking a step back, breaking free from his urgent hold.

"About what?"

"Everything." She took a seat upon the moist rocks, to rest her quivering legs. "What we haven't had time to talk about."

"I'm not sure what you mean." Nick sat beside her. She'd lost his eyes again.

"What was building between us," Cassie said softly. "While Adam was gone."

In the moonlight Cassie could see Nick's carven, handsome features with their hint of defensiveness.

"I think it was a confusing time for both of us," Cassie said as honestly as she could. "We've always had a connection, Nick, and we probably always will. But that doesn't mean . . ." She couldn't finish her sentence.

Cassie couldn't ignore the depth of Nick's feelings for her, not when his love was so strong it allowed him to fight his possession. But she would be lying if she said that what she felt for him was equally as strong, or the same.

"I know I haven't been fair to you," she continued. "You were there for me when I needed you, in a way no one else has been. But Adam is my one true love. I have to let you go, for real this time."

Nick's jaw tightened. She'd caught him completely off guard by being so blunt. In fact, she'd caught herself off guard as well.

"I think we may be facing the end, Nick, all of us. Once the ancestors have eternal life, they're likely to unleash another bubonic plague on the world. It's more important than ever for us not to be distracted.

"I really do love you," she added, after a few seconds of uncomfortable silence. "But not the same way I love Adam. And you deserve someone who loves you that way."

Nick nodded, stone-faced, and then brushed off Cassie's words in his usual manner. "I'll get over it," he said, as if their moment was nothing. "What we should be thinking about right now is Faye. Look at that moon."

He pointed at the sky. "That's our stopwatch."

Cassie didn't allow herself to glimpse the waxing gibbous moon another time. It was too terrifying to look at.

"If only we could catch Faye in a moment of weakness," he said. "But she's never weak. She's Faye."

It was true, Cassie thought. The last time Faye had allowed herself to be vulnerable was—

Of course.

Cassie snapped to attention. The sound of the ocean was crisp in her ears. It was whispering to her, sharing its deeply hidden secrets.

"What is it?" Nick asked.

"I know just the place," Cassie said. "To catch Faye with her heart open."

CHAPTER 23

Cassie stepped across the crooked stream and around the few small ponds that led to Suzan's grave. It was evening but still light as day, barely a shadow upon the ground.

Even from afar, Cassie could see that Suzan's head-stone was whiter and cleaner than those surrounding it. It was newer. The dirt it stood upon was just sprouting with freshly planted grass. It would take weeks for the tiny green pinpoints to grow as long and lush as the adjoining lawn. As Cassie expected, Faye was there, standing over the stone. She'd wrapped herself in a knit black shawl, even though the breeze tonight was warm and summery and the humidity high.

One evening a while back Cassie had come upon Faye in just this spot by accident, but she left her undisturbed. She'd understood at the time that mourning Suzan's death was a process Faye needed to go through on her own. But after that encounter, it didn't take long for Cassie to notice that Faye visited there every week at the same time, on the anniversary of Suzan's death.

Tonight was no different. Cassie approached her quietly and respectfully. It took a few moments for Faye to turn around. When she did, Cassie noticed her eyes were red rimmed and soft. She quickly wiped a long-tailed tear from her cheek.

"What are you doing here?" she asked, her voice sounding hoarse and raspy.

The warm breeze rustled the foliage over their heads, and Cassie began speaking before Faye had the chance to react more harshly. "Death is a terrible, frightening thing, isn't it?" she said.

Faye stared out into the distance to the east, where the coastline was visible. She didn't reply, but she also made no move to run away.

Cassie continued talking. "But eternal life isn't the solution to what happened with Suzan. Dark powers won't bring her back, Faye, you know that. And losing Suzan only proves just how much we need each other right now."

Faye began shaking her head, so Cassie spoke louder and faster. "The ancestors are manipulating you into believing they really care about you, but they don't. All they care about is—"

"Enough already," Faye said, cutting Cassie off. "Do you really think I don't already know all that?"

Her tone was condescending but not outraged. It sounded to Cassie, well, almost *sensible*.

"That's why I went over to the other side to begin with," Faye said. "I was the only one who could do it without suspicion."

"I don't understand," Cassie said.

Faye's expression, framed by a background of rolling hills and granite cliffs, completely altered. She brought her voice down to a whisper.

"I went to their side to spy on them. I couldn't go back with you all because I didn't have enough information, and I didn't want to blow my cover."

Cassie was taken aback. "Do you mean—"

"I outsmarted all of you," Faye said. "Aren't you used to it by now?"

Cassie tried to look past Faye's cocky surface, to decipher if she was telling the truth.

"As I suspected, the ancestors are a bunch of backstabbers," Faye continued. "I thought it all along, but now I have proof."

She glanced left and right. "I found something at the warehouse. A small glass bottle that contains a lock of Scarlett's hair and some other things. Her fingernails, a drop of blood, and a piece of hematite, which is Scarlett's working stone. It's bespelled, Cassie. And if the ancestors smash it to the ground, Scarlett will be stripped of her powers."

Cassie was quiet for a few seconds, shocked that even the ancestors would stoop so low, but also feeling a little ashamed. Cassie had been so quick to assume the worst about Faye.

"I underestimated you," she said. "I'm sorry."

"I knew you would." Faye let her eyes drop to Suzan's grave. "That's how I was sure my plan would work."

Cassie had the urge to give Faye a hug, but she knew better than to try. "She'd be proud of you," she said instead, placing a hand on Suzan's headstone.

Faye looked away, but Cassie noticed a solitary tear fall from her chin onto the fresh grass.

"I'll steal the bottle," she said, "and come to your house tonight. Time's just about up."

~~~~~~

Faye sat on the edge of what used to be her bed in the secret room, soaking in all the attention. The Circle listened in awe as she described every detail of the previous few days—how she'd managed to fool everyone.

"This calls for a celebration," Chris said. "A party on the beach. It's been so long since we went night swimming."

Even Cassie got swept into the idea. This *was* cause for celebration, wasn't it? She was about to run for her swimsuit when Nick let out a deep, aggravated breath.

"I know getting Faye back feels like a big victory to the Circle," he said. "And it is, but it doesn't automatically solve any of our problems."

He passed his severe eyes over each of them. "We're not in the clear just yet. We need to destroy these ancestors, and we need Scarlett to do it. Remember?"

Faye sprang up from the bed and took charge of the floor. "Nick is absolutely right," she said. "And fortunately I've learned some things during my Oscar-worthy performance as a double agent."

She held her head high as she waited for everyone to

begin listening intently. "Eternal life is what the ancestors have been after all along," she said. "First they needed to be resurrected. Scarlett did that for them, but she also tried to set herself up as their leader. And that was her fatal mistake. They don't think she's even worthy of being a Blak. Cassie's the one they wanted. She's the stronger sister."

Faye paused to let her words sink in. "The ancestors are only using Scarlett to get eternal life, but as soon as they have it, they plan to betray her."

"Untrustworthy demons, go figure," Sean called out.

Faye began prowling the room like a panther. "They don't like the idea that Scarlett tried to situate herself as their boss. They see her as a greedy young girl, a know-it-all."

Faye went for her bag and carefully pulled out the small glass bottle she had told Cassie about. It was corked tightly with a rubber stopper. "Once the ancestors perform the eternal-life spell, they're going to smash this bottle to the ground, stripping Scarlett of her powers forever."

She held the bottle up high for everyone to see.

"I went along with their plan," she said. "I didn't say anything because then they'd turn on me, too. But I can promise you that Scarlett has no idea how much the ancestors resent her."

"She's got it coming," Deborah said.

Chris agreed. "We should let them hurt her. It's what she deserves."

Cassie thought back to the scene of Scarlett and all the ancestors having dinner together at the warehouse. Scarlett had been so content in that moment, foolishly so.

"All Scarlett wants is to feel connected," Cassie shouted out. "To have these ancestors be her family. That's why she's so blind to their deception—she wants to believe in the best of them."

"Well, poor Scarlett," Doug said, pretending to wipe away tears.

"Don't you see?" Cassie said. "That's our in."

Cassie reached out for the glass bottle. "I'm going to talk to Scarlett and show her this."

Faye handed it over without argument.

"Why can't we all go?" Melanie asked.

But Cassie only repeated herself, examining the tiny but dangerous bottle in the palm of her hand. "I'm going to talk to her, sister to sister."

CHAPTER 24

Cassie glanced at the time on her cell phone. She was sitting on a green wooden bench watching kids play on a jungle gym. Mothers pushed their toddlers on a squeaky swing set. She'd arranged to meet Scarlett here at the public park to talk, but it had been almost an hour and she was still waiting. She checked the time on her cell phone again and mentally rehearsed her speech. But it was all beginning to feel like a wasted effort if Scarlett wouldn't be there to hear it.

The group of children Cassie had been watching were ushered away, immediately replaced with a new set—uniformly loud and rambunctious, and equally doted upon by protective parents and nannies. Sometimes Cassie looked at children like these, with their heedless innocence and their unconditional love, and she wondered, *Was I ever like that?*

But the thing was, she wasn't. That version of childhood had never been available to her.

Kind of like sisterhood, she thought. Self-pitying or not, Cassie had been shortchanged on both. And here she was, still not having learned her lesson, still trying for what she could never have.

Just as Cassie was about to give up, Scarlett appeared beside her. Maybe she'd been watching out of sight, testing Cassie to see how long she could keep her waiting before she'd give up and go home. She was wearing blue jeans, a white T-shirt, and her favorite brown bowler hat. There was no apology for arriving more than an hour late.

"Have you been sitting here awhile?" she asked. "You've got a little sunburn on your nose. With your fair skin, Cassie, you should really be more careful of the sun."

Cassie's patience had been worn thin. With Scarlett and her oversize attitude hovering in her face now, she had the urge to lash out at her. All the mental preparations of the past hour had slipped right away, all the rehearsing of every perfect word had been replaced by a tingling in her gut and the itch to knock Scarlett right back down to size.

"Before you start shooting your mouth off," Scarlett said, "just know that you can't convince me to leave my Circle. Even though you've got Faye on your side right now, we'll get someone else to cross over."

Cassie silently counted backward from a hundred to remain calm.

Scarlett joined Cassie on the bench and observed the kids at play. "What a bunch of brats," she said flippantly. "I never want kids."

"I asked you here today to warn you," Cassie said, giving no credence to Scarlett's attempt at levity. "It's not our Circle that's against you, it's your own."

Scarlett rolled her dark eyes. "Here we go," she said.

"I'm telling you the truth," Cassie insisted. "The ancestors plan to strip you of your power once they have eternal life."

"And you know this *how*, exactly?" Scarlett asked, giddy with sarcasm.

"They confided in Faye," Cassie said. "Once they have what they need, they won't hesitate to dispose of you."

"No." Scarlett shook her head. "I don't believe you.

They're my family. They're *our* family, Cassie. If only you'd let yourself see it."

Cassie thought again of Scarlett's dinner with the ancestors. How hard she was trying to build a home out of that dilapidated warehouse—a kitchen, a living room, a treasured dining table and chairs from discarded, long-forgotten castoffs. Maybe the two of them weren't so different. They both had so much empty space to fill within them.

"You and I are each other's family," Cassie said. "They're nothing more than our selfish, evil ancestors who don't care about us."

She could see Scarlett was having a hard time accepting this brutal truth. "Think about it," she said. "They've been dead for centuries. They have no humanity left in them. Imagine being stripped of your power—or worse. Is that a gamble you want to take?"

Scarlett opened her mouth indignantly and then closed it again. "You're lying."

"If I'm lying, then why do I have this?" Cassie opened her bag and carefully pulled out the glass bottle.

Scarlett froze at the sight of it.

"Faye took this from the warehouse," Cassie said. "That's your hair, your blood."

Scarlett took the bottle from Cassie and examined it. Her dyed red locks were unmistakable.

"I understand the importance of building a family," Cassie said. "But they're using you, Scarlett, and you deserve better than that."

Scarlett cupped the bottle gently with both hands and brought it into her lap. For a moment the sound of a child's laughter drowned out every other sound. It was immediately followed by another child's crying.

All the meanness escaped Scarlett's face. "But they're so much more powerful than we are, Cassie. Even if I join your side, there's no stopping them."

"Yes, there is." Cassie felt the crushing sense of helplessness she'd been experiencing for days slightly rise, but it was a tenuous moment. *This is it*, she thought. *Don't mess this up now.*

"I have a spell," she said, "that we can use to burn our father's Book of Shadows and destroy everything that's come from it. Including the ancestors. We'll be free of all of it forever."

"Where'd you get this spell?" Scarlett asked defensively, but Cassie sensed a tinge of hope in her voice.

"From an old witch," Cassie answered. "Our father stripped him of his power years ago. It's a spell he created."

"And you trust him?" Scarlett asked.

"It'll be dangerous; he told me as much. It's never been performed before. But I believe it'll work—with your help."

"You *believe* or you *hope?*" Scarlett asked.

"Both, I guess," Cassie answered.

She joined Scarlett in staring forward for a moment. "Timothy knows a lot about our family. If this spell wasn't something our father feared, he wouldn't have had to strip him of his magic."

Together Cassie and Scarlett watched two toddlers in matching blond pigtails each pulling on the arm of a plastic doll. Both girls were hysterical, tears the size of winter hail tumbling from their eyes. Seconds before, the toy had just been lying on the grass, ignored. Their father had to step in to mediate. He yanked the doll from both their hands, tossed it out of sight, and then distracted his daughters from their grief by guiding them, hands held, to the monkey bars. Just like that, their anguish was forgotten. The tears were still wet on their cheeks as their faces brightened.

Cassie turned to Scarlett. It wasn't lost on either of them that they'd missed out on something crucial in not having a proper father or sister.

Scarlett choked back tears, and Cassie realized a hard

knot was forming in her own throat as well. She had to strive to keep herself dry-eyed.

"I guess you're all I have left, Cassie," Scarlett said. "You're my only chance of saving myself. How's that for pathetic?"

Cassie reached for Scarlett's hand and squeezed it in her own. "We're each other's only chance, Scarlett. Pathetic or not."

CHAPTER 25

In the dark of night, the group walked upward, past all the other houses on Crowhaven Road, including Cassie's house at Number Twelve. When they reached the highest point, it looked just as Cassie remembered it. Timothy's spell called for performing the book-burning outdoors, on grounds that would have had some significance to Black John, so here they were at the ultimate point on the headland, where Black John's ruined house used to sit, Number Thirteen. It was the last place Cassie ever wanted to be. She walked to the cliff's edge and stared down at the waves below.

The Circle stepped over and around the bits of

foundation left over from the razed house. Cassie had brought three things with her: Black John's Book of Shadows, a sack containing the Master Tools, and the wooden boxes Timothy had given her.

Scarlett, Faye, Diana, and Adam kneeled down closest to Cassie as she unclasped the larger box's brass latches and lifted its heavy top.

Cassie unpacked its contents: robes, crystals, incense, and candles; a black-handled dagger, a spade, and some wooden logs. Then she found a tiny vial of clear liquid that could have been holy water but she understood was a potion. Lining the bottom of the box was a yellowed piece of paper that contained detailed pictorial instructions on how to prepare the spell, but no words. Probably so anyone from any time, a speaker of any language, could read and understand it. Timothy had thought of everything.

"These robes are handmade," Laurel said. "They're beautiful." They were pagan ritual robes of various styles, from many different centuries. Black, red, green, purple. There were twelve of them in all, one for each member of the Circle.

Once everyone else had put one on, there was one robe left. It was white with gold trim. The creases in its pristine cloth were crisp and sharp.

"That one's yours, Cassie," Diana said. "It goes to the spell master leading the ritual."

Cassie felt lofty and proud as she slipped one arm, and then the other, through the robe's soft cotton sleeves. Faye reached for the black-handled dagger.

"An Athame," she said, sliding the blade from its sheath. "It's so old, and solid. And sharp."

"A what?" Sean asked.

Laurel took the dagger from Faye's hands and examined it. "The Athame knife is reserved for special ceremonies and rituals," she said. "It's used for summoning or banishing spirit entities."

Deborah reached for the knife, but Laurel wouldn't give it up.

"If it's a proper Athame," she continued, "when it's used to draw the circle at the beginning of a ritual, it can cast away negative energies like a shield."

"Well, it had better be a proper Athame then, because that's exactly what we're going to need," Scarlett said. She flipped through the different forms of incense that came out of the box. "Golden copal, dragon's blood, pine and cedar," she said. "This Timothy guy didn't leave anything out."

Melanie gathered together a multicolored heap of

crystals. They were all different shapes and sizes. She pointed out a stack of flesh-colored candles. "Those are incredibly rare," she said. "Made with tallow, the fat from cows or sheep."

Nick picked up the wooden spade. "I'll do the digging," he said. "For the fire pit."

Cassie observed the medieval-looking tool in his hand. It resembled an axe, with a T handle, pointed toward the tip.

Adam reached for the logs, which were seasoned oak, and the vial of liquid that would be used as lighter fluid. "I'll help," he said to Nick. The two of them calculated what would be the center point of the foundation.

Diana, Faye, and Cassie each put on one of the Master Tools.

Cassie looked up at the almost-full moon. It looked like an oddly formed egg, an imperfect oval. She listened to the waves crashing at the base of the cliff they stood upon. In her arms she clutched the book. It felt warm against her skin, needy and alive, like a loving child.

It isn't real, she told herself. The affection she felt emitting from the book wasn't love; it was darkness, temptation, the embodiment of everything she had to fight against.

She set the book down for the moment, inside Timothy's now-empty box, and focused on her friends as they prepared the spell.

Laurel held the instructions with both hands as Melanie laid out the proper formation of crystals to enhance the flow of energy from the ground to the air. Sean, Chris, and Doug lit the candles and incense, cleansing the space with swinging censers.

Nick's hands and arms grew filthy as he dug a deep circular pit into the ground. Adam and Deborah lined it with a crosshatch of logs.

Diana came into view, beautiful and majestic in her sunlight-colored robe and sparkling diadem. Faye gleamed in red beneath the moon, with the garter tight around her leg.

Cassie imagined what she looked like in her white and gold robe, with the silver bracelet shining upon her arm. She wished she could see herself in this imperative moment, as she and her friends were on the brink of rewriting the course of their history—their future.

Cassie gripped the dagger's cool handle and stabbed it into the hard, dry dirt. She drew a deep circle around the ruined foundation, encircling the wood-filled pit with a wide ring.

Silently, everyone stepped inside to the inner perimeter of the circle, and Cassie closed it shut.

Adam handed Cassie the vial of clear fluid. Cassie lifted its cap and poured its contents out over the logs. Next Adam handed her a lit match. She held it up to her eyes for only a second before letting it slip from her fingers.

The fire blazed into flames not unlike wild demons newly unleashed from the ground.

Cassie turned toward the eastern sky and held up both her arms. "I call on the Watchtower of the East," she shouted. "Powers of Air, protect us."

In a few seconds a gentle breeze blew through her hair and around the circle, fueling the fire with new life.

Next Cassie turned southward. "I call on the Watchtower of the South," she said. "Powers of Fire, protect us."

She closed her eyes and felt the heat of the high flames on her face.

Then Cassie turned again. "I call on the Watchtower of the West," she said. "Powers of Water, protect us."

The waves in the distance below them crashed loudly upon the shore, and the strong briny smell of the ocean rose up to fill their lungs.

Finally, Cassie faced north. "Watchtower of the North," she said. "Powers of Earth, protect us."

The ground beneath their feet suddenly began to quake. The book rumbled. Cassie could feel herself breathing hard. The circle she'd cut into the soil with the dagger split from the rest of the foundation, leaving them standing on an island of ragged dirt.

Then she gazed into the flames that flailed from deep within the pit, and harnessed her energy. This was it. She closed her eyes.

But then someone gasped, and someone else choked.

Cassie opened her eyes and quickly turned around. Alice was charging toward them, and close behind her the rest of the ancestors advanced across the empty lot like an army of ghosts.

"They must have followed me," Scarlett said.

Cassie's friends were gasping for air. Sean, Chris, and Doug were the first to collapse, but all of them except Cassie and Scarlett were gripping their necks, suffocating.

Scarlett raised her hands and performed a spell to restore their breath. But by then the ancestors had reached the Circle, close enough to knock Sean, Chris, and Doug out with an even stronger suffocation spell.

Adam and Nick launched an attack, a binding spell to

constrain the ancestors' strength, but Absolom shielded it easily, with the help of Thomas and Samuel. They retaliated with a hard stare that threw both Adam and Nick violently onto the ground. Adam hit the dirt with a *thud* and was immediately knocked unconscious. Nick landed gruesomely on a protruding beam from the ruined foundation of the house. It stabbed straight through his upper thigh, impaling the flesh like a thick, rusty skewer. He cried out in pain. The sight of his blood weakened Cassie at the knees.

Alice targeted Diana and Deborah. Melanie and Laurel tried to protect them with a defense spell, but all four of them dropped lifelessly beneath Alice's open hand.

Faye lifted her hands and focused her energy on Alice. She managed to steer Alice back, away from her friends, but only long enough to attract Charlotte's attention.

Charlotte gestured toward Faye and sent her flying backward into the air. Cassie and Scarlett were the only two Circle members left standing.

The ancestors surrounded them.

"Our brethren," Alice said. "We left you for last."

Beatrix grabbed Scarlett by the neck and pulled her face close to her own. "You, we'll kill," she said, "while you"—she signaled to Cassie—"watch."

Absolom placed his palm over Scarlett's forehead. He whispered words Cassie didn't recognize.

"Then you'll be ours," Alice said to Cassie. "At last."

"*I maledicentibus vobis in mortem,*" Absolom mumbled over Scarlett's forehead. "*I maledicentibus vobis in mortem.*"

If not for Beatrix holding Scarlett's thin body up, she would have slid to the ground. Her wide eyes glassed over, and her neck drooped down. Her face became a mask. Cassie understood what she was witnessing all too well: Scarlett was beginning to die.

Cassie raised her arms to harness her energy, to go inward and find a spell, but Alice's gaze left her mind blank, powerless. Her spells, even her dark magic, were just out of her own reach.

She surveyed the surrounding area. Her friends lay scattered, unmoving. She couldn't be sure who was alive, if any.

Then Cassie caught sight of something else. The wooden box Timothy had given her. The one he had said not to open until she had no other choice.

This had to be that moment.

Cassie dashed for the box before Alice or any of the ancestors could stop her. She kneeled down beside it, unlatched its hinges, and lifted its top.

Cassie drew back at the sight of its contents.

Rats. Dead rats, piled on top of one another in a mass grave of matted fur and desiccated tails. One whiff of their putrid scent made Cassie gag. She stood up and backed away from the box. Was this some sick joke? Was Timothy on the ancestors' side all along?

Cassie glanced back at the ancestors still hovering over Scarlett. Alice watched Cassie, unafraid, unthreatened, confident there was nowhere for her to run to.

Then Cassie heard a squeak, followed by a scratching. She peered cautiously over the top of the wooden box. What seemed like a thousand beady, blinking eyes stared back at her. Their bodies began to twist and move, slinking free from their entanglement. Cassie held her breath as the whole herd of them scurried out over the top of their box and raced for the ancestors.

Their long rodent tails dragged behind them as they charged for whatever exposed skin they found—the vulnerable flesh of ankles and calves. Scratching and clawing, the leader of the pack leapt for the nearest target first: Alice. She lifted her hands in defense, but her fingers only provided an easier-to-reach mark.

The rest of the squealing herd hurried up the length of the ancestors' legs. They bit at their faces, gnawed on the soft, chewy lobes of their ears.

Absolom shrieked and abandoned his spell, thrashing. Beatrix released Scarlett and struggled to shake her limbs free of the teeth-clenching vermin. She flailed like a person on fire.

Samuel scrambled to pick up a broken metal rod from the ground, a remnant of the house's foundation. He swung it hard and wide in an arc, like a baseball bat, but was successful in fighting off the rats for only a moment before being overcome. He soon fell beneath a hungry, squealing mountain of fur and tails, just like the others.

Cassie rushed to Scarlett. She listened for her breath and felt for her pulse. She was alive, but barely. Cassie strived to concentrate in spite of her surroundings, to recall a spell to restore Scarlett's energy. She placed her hands over her body and waited for the words to come. When they did, she whispered them softly: *"Recuperabit, reddere, renovare."*

Scarlett groaned, then opened her eyes, and the color returned to her cheeks. She took a deep breath and climbed to her feet.

"Oh, my god," she said, at the horrible sight of the ancestors.

They'd managed to ward off the rats, so they were no longer being devoured, but the damage had been done.

Thomas's clothes had been chewed through to pieces. His skin showed through the shredded cloth, bloody and oozing. All of the ancestors' skin was pockmarked and pusfilled. The whites of their eyes had yellowed, and their breathing was slack.

Charlotte bent over and coughed, and a black sludge poured out of her mouth.

Cassie noticed the tips of Alice's fingers were blackening, and so were her lips.

"What's happening to them?" Scarlett asked.

Absolom and Beatrix were next to double over and retch putrid mucus into a dark, wet pile on the ground.

"The Black Death," Cassie said.

The rats banded together in a tight pack, eyes ablaze, their mouths foaming with blood. They scurried back to their wooden box, twitching and satisfied.

"Those weren't just any rats." Cassie threw the top back over the box and observed the ancestors writhing in pain, heaving, spitting, their limbs rotting to deadened stumps.

"The bubonic plague just came back to bite them," Cassie said to Scarlett. It looked worse than she'd ever imagined.

But the ancestors weren't giving up that easily. They

crawled across the dirt to clasp hands. They were pooling their energy.

Cassie wouldn't put it past them to overcome even this. "We have to finish the spell," she said. "Get everyone together."

Scarlett helped Diana and Faye up to standing position. Adam, Sean, and the Hendersons rose of their own accord.

Cassie hurried over to Nick. He'd lost a lot of blood, and his skin felt cold to the touch, but his eyes were open. He tried to talk, but Cassie quieted him.

"Just relax," she said. "You're going to be okay." She held her hands over his injury and searched her mind for the right spell.

"I don't need magic." Nick's voice was raspy but forceful. "I only need you." He reached for her hand and squeezed it.

Cassie could see that the injury to his leg was serious. Nick was in shock. Magic was the only chance of saving him.

Cassie hovered her free hand over the spear of metal impaled through the flesh, and silently cast a spell: *Periculosum metallic tutum esse liberum.*

The hole in Nick's leg opened like a mouth, releasing

the metal beam to the air. It rose and fell to his side, into the red pool of his blood.

"I'm okay," Nick insisted. "I can get up. Don't waste your energy on me. You have a spell to cast."

Resanesco, Cassie thought. *Resanesco*.

Nick stirred as the wound stitched itself sealed, cleanly. Still squeezing Cassie's hand, he lifted his head just high enough to catch a glimpse of his injury.

"It's not even as bad as I thought," he said.

Cassie inhaled a thankful breath. Nick would be okay. She was about to help him up when a new string of words entered her mind.

Let him feel the love I have for him, and let it be enough. She said them to herself silently, just as she had the others.

"Thank you, Cassie," Nick said, rolling over onto his side. "But I'm really fine."

"Hurry up!" Scarlett called out. She'd managed to get everyone else in formation. The ancestors were still trying to regain their strength.

Cassie helped Nick to his feet and led him to the Circle. When they stepped into place, the fire began to smolder. Gray smoke rose from its source, darker and darker, until it formed a coal-black cloud overhead.

Cassie picked up her father's book from its place on the

ground. She held it up high for all her friends to see. Then she held it over the fire and allowed the spell to come:

> *I cast you out, unclean spirit, in the name of goodness.*
> *All sources of light and truth, we appeal to you and your sacred boundless power.*
> *Be gone, darkness. Leave us a dwelling place of light.*
> *We renounce you, all symbols of darkness, demons, and all evil.*

The fire hissed and sizzled. Red-hot embers shot up like sparkles from the flames.

For a moment Cassie had a thought: What if she didn't drop the book into the fire? What if the infected rats had accomplished enough to weaken the ancestors? Maybe they were soon to die anyway. Then Cassie and her Circle could have the best of both worlds—she could keep the book without her relatives trying to control it.

One by one, the ancestors climbed to their feet and struggled toward the circle's perimeter. Their sickened eyes were furious and helpless as they watched and waited for what Cassie would do next. Blood dripped from their noses and ears.

The book called to Cassie. It screamed her name. She

pulled it back slightly from the heat of the flames. This book was her past, she thought. It was her last and final connection to her father and to her lineage.

It felt like a living precious diamond in her hands. A one-of-a-kind power. Could she really just cast it away? Destroy it forever?

No. She couldn't.

She took one giant step back from the fire and hugged the book tightly, embracing it over her heart. It had a heartbeat, too, she realized—its own. And their two hearts beat together as one.

All other sound drifted up and away. Only the book existed to Cassie now. And then he spoke to her.

"Cassandra, my one and only," he said. *Him.* Her father.

His voice was like a poison that seized Cassie's throat.

"Don't disappoint the long line of witches that brought you here," he said. "The witches that made you. They are all you have."

Cassie's pulse quickened. She couldn't catch her breath.

"All their knowledge is yours," he said. "Their power is yours. Don't throw it away."

Everything began to spin. Cassie lost all sense of up

from down, left from right. Her own body felt like nothing. An empty shell.

"Don't turn your back on your past," her father said.
"Destroying that book will destroy who you really are."

Who am I? Cassie thought.

*I am Cassandra Blake, child of Alexandra and John,
beloved daughter, loving friend.*

I am power.

But I can surrender that power to the flames.

If I have power without love, I have nothing.

Something inside Cassie's mind clicked. If evil was
what she really was, who she really was, then so be it. Let
evil be destroyed. Let light triumph over darkness once
and for all.

A feeling of warmth enveloped her like daybreak.

She shouted the final words of the spell: "Depart, evil
spirits. Leave this good and innocent world!"

Cassie lifted the book up and heaved it into the fire.
"Depart, Father!" she screamed out. "Depart!"

Her father's cry rang out for all to hear.

The ancestors could do nothing to stop her. The
moment the book hit the flames their bodies stiffened,
and as it burned, they burned.

Flames penetrated the ancestors' chests as if the fire

started in their hearts and spread upward and out from there. Their mouths softened as they wailed. Noses liquefied, eyes dissolved. The ground beneath their melting bodies broiled and withered. Alice moved her head from side to side on her shoulders. Her face took on a mournful expression as she stretched her neck and cried out. The grief-stricken sound seemed to ricochet off the moon.

The fire pit popped.

The book glowed orange like a lit coal. From its flame-engulfed pages, Cassie's father's scream went quiet. It was their final requiem. Scarlett, Cassie noticed, had begun to tremble. A darkness drained from her eyes and mouth like a black, smoky mist.

The wind stirred, making a rushing sound through the air. It carried with it a strange sense of change.

Cassie stared down into the fire, and it suddenly seemed to be everywhere. Far and wide, hers was the only screaming voice now. It echoed from within the center of the flames. *I'm in the fire*, Cassie thought. *I am it.*

When it exploded, an ashy mist rose like a mushroom cloud, throwing Cassie skyward.

She landed flat with her arms wide open to her sides. There was an unnatural warmth to her face and a heaviness in the air. She sat up, blinked her eyes, and looked around.

Only her Circle remained. All else was gone: the ancestors, the book, even the fire.

They'd done it. In her soul, Cassie knew they had won.

The Circle gathered around her, bending, leaning.

"Cassie?" Adam said. He was staring at her strangely. So was Diana.

"Are you okay?" one of them said, just before everything went soft and gray, and all Cassie saw was darkness.

<hr>

Cassie reopened her eyes to the Circle huddled around her. Adam was holding her hand.

She sat up slowly, weak and woozy. "I feel different," she said. "Do any of you feel different?"

Adam told her to keep calm, that the spell must have been too much for her.

"Nobody else feels different?" she asked. "Scarlett?"

Scarlett's face appeared airy and open. "I do," she said. "I feel good."

But Cassie didn't feel *good*. There was a new void in herself, an emptiness. She felt *powerless*.

She got up on her feet and focused her energy on a small round rock upon the ground. It was the simplest spell she could think of, to try and make it rise. She focused every ounce of energy she had on that little pebble, and nothing happened. It didn't budge.

"Timothy warned us that there would be consequences," she said.

"Cassie, what are you talking about?" Adam asked.

"There needed to be a sacrifice," Cassie said. "And it was me. I've lost my magic."

CHAPTER 26

"Let's just get you home, Cassie," Adam said. *"Everyone else* can take care of cleaning up."

Cassie didn't have the strength to decline, so she made a motion toward the bluff. Adam put his arm around her shoulders and guided her along. Cassie didn't offer much more than a nod good-bye to her friends, but they seemed to understand.

Only Scarlett ran after them. "Wait," she said. "I have to tell you something."

Cassie stopped and turned.

Adam tensed up. "Can't it wait?"

"I'm sorry, but it can't." Scarlett spoke almost directly

to the ground. "The cord that you saw, Cassie. The one between Adam and me. It was just a ruse."

Cassie felt her heart skip a beat.

"A ruse?" Adam said for both of them.

Scarlett nodded. "It was a visualization spell that I cast. It wasn't real. I was just trying to tear Cassie down however I could."

Cassie let this truth settle over her like ash. It felt like both a final moment of destruction and a cleansing rebirth. Scarlett continued talking.

"I realize now that it was the darkness controlling me all along," she said. "I was out of control. And I'm so ashamed."

Cassie closed her eyes for a moment. She couldn't decipher if the trembling in her chest was happiness or anger or sadness. She'd had so many doubts about Adam these past weeks because of something that was a lie.

"I don't know what to say," she mumbled. "I need some space right now, Scarlett."

Cassie ventured toward the beach. She heard Adam tell Scarlett to head back to the others, to help clean up. Then he chased after Cassie.

He caught her by her hand, pulled her in toward him, but at the sight of her face he faltered.

Why wasn't she smiling?

Cassie turned to the water. Only a gentle wind was blowing, but it felt to her like a frigid gust beating against her skin.

"I knew it," Adam said to the back of her head. "I told you. I never doubted for a second that you were my one and only soul mate."

But Cassie did have doubts. She'd been so fooled by a fake cord that she almost let Adam go.

She wanted to feel moved now, to be calmed. But everything hurt too much.

She'd heard her father's voice calling out from the book, warning her not to turn her back on her past. He told her that destroying the book would destroy who she really was. And it had.

Her power was gone. She'd surrendered it to the flames—and she knew! She had known, somewhere deep inside herself, that this would happen. It was a decision she had made. *If I have power without love*, she'd thought, *I have nothing*. If evil was what she was, who she was . . . she chose to sacrifice it all to the fire.

Now she had to live with that choice forever.

Adam held Cassie from behind, by the shoulders. "Aren't you the slightest bit relieved the cord was just a trick?"

She was, but it seemed almost beside the point under these new circumstances. *Love without power*, she thought. *If I have love without power, do I still have nothing?*

"I've lost my magic, Adam," she said, turning to face him. "Do you not understand that?"

Adam averted his eyes.

"Now our Circle is unbound." Cassie found herself frantically worrying aloud. "And you might need to replace me. A loss of magic would probably have different terms than death, so it might not necessarily have to be a replacement of bloodline."

Adam cautiously placed his hand upon Cassie's shoulder. "Calm down," he said. "You're getting ahead of yourself. Maybe there's a way we can get your powers back."

He brought Cassie in for a warm, firm embrace. "And I hope you know that I will stand by your side, no matter what happens."

Of course Adam would. Cassie didn't doubt that for a second. But he was refusing to acknowledge certain facts. A powerless witch was a liability.

She pulled away from Adam's hug and looked out at the ocean spanning in front of her. She thought of Timothy, on his own and driven mad by not being able to practice witchcraft. That was the lonely, discouraged fate of a powerless witch—they were better off alone, better off isolated than to drag everyone around them under with their frustration.

Cassie wouldn't say so out loud, but she wondered if there might be a better place for her than New Salem after all.

She turned and began walking toward her house again. Adam loyally trailed behind her, having given up on trying to make her talk, on trying to get her to look on the bright side. But he followed her the whole way home.

For the first time since they'd met, Cassie knew that Adam couldn't understand what she was going through. He could never comprehend how sometimes love, even true love, just wasn't enough.

CHAPTER 27

Cassie was slumped in the leather recliner in the corner. She hadn't even wanted to attend this meeting, but coming and zoning out seemed easier than formulating a decent excuse to miss it. She stared at the modern artwork that decorated the walls of Diana's living room. Abstract lines in black and gray and beige. Completely bereft of emotion, like she felt at the moment. Dead inside.

The group discussed their situation—an unbound Circle and a powerless Cassie—in hushed tones. What Cassie noticed in their quiet voices wasn't compassion so much as pity. None of them could even look at her.

"We have to figure out what the heck to do now," Scarlett said.

Max was seated beside Diana on the couch. "There must be a spell you all can do. Isn't there a spell for just about everything?"

Laurel shook her head. "Not everything."

"So we have an unbound Circle," Sean said. "So what? We've already beaten all our enemies."

Deborah cracked her knuckles. "There will always be more enemies."

"That's not the point," Adam called out. "Cassie will never feel like herself again without her power. And she deserves to . . ." He paused, and his cheeks flushed. "Well, she deserves to feel like herself. I'd give her all my power if only I could."

"If only," Melanie said. "I would, too."

"That's it." Diana had a stroke of inspiration that brought her right off the couch.

"Cassie," she said, turning to her. "Timothy muttered something that time we saw him that I haven't been able to get out of my head. About no one being willing to give him their power after he'd lost his."

"I remember that, too," Adam said.

Cassie did recall Timothy's comment, but she hadn't thought much about it at the time. "So?" she said.

"That means power can be transferred from one witch to another." Diana sprinted to her bedroom to retrieve her Book of Shadows.

She returned to the room a minute later, flipping through its pages so quickly, Cassie feared the delicate old paper might get torn. "I think I saw a spell like that once."

Diana was nearly frantic with new hope, but Cassie felt hardly any. If Timothy, who was brilliant and old and wise, hadn't figured out how to get his powers back after all these years, how could Cassie expect to?

"This is it," Diana said, finally finding what she was looking for. "It's a variation of a binding spell."

Everyone leaned forward as Diana silently read over the text.

"A group of witches can pool their energy and life force together," she said, looking up. "And offer it to another witch."

"So this is a way for Cassie to get her power back?" Scarlett asked.

Diana read over the text again. "She'd be given a small

amount of power from everyone willing to bind themselves to her."

She glanced at Cassie. "Timothy's problem was that no one was willing to give up any power to him."

Melanie spoke up before the group could prematurely celebrate. "It's a lot to ask," she said. "Anyone who participates would be choosing to make themselves weaker so Cassie can become stronger."

"Just a tiny bit weaker, though, right?" Faye asked.

"We're already bound to each other through the Circle," Adam said. "Shifting some of that to Cassie might not make a big difference."

Diana crossed the room to Cassie's recliner. She sat on its wide leather arm. "I'm willing to give it a try," she said. "But it might take even more than our Circle to gather enough magic to get Cassie back to normal."

"We can ask the elders," Laurel said. "My grandma Quincey and Adam's grandmother, old Mrs. Franklin. And don't forget about Cassie's mom."

"There are all of our parents," Diana said. "The ones who are still alive."

Faye tensed at this idea. "Our parents haven't performed magic in almost twenty years. They'd rather go on pretending they don't have powers."

"We've come this far without their help," Sean said. "We don't need to start asking for it now."

"I agree." Deborah was as resentful of their parents' generation as Faye was. "Between the eleven of us and the old crones, we'll give Cassie all that we can. Our parents could never be counted on to come through."

The room fell silent at last, and all eyes turned to Cassie for her reaction.

But Cassie's feelings seemed to be on a delay, like someone had carved out the parts of her brain responsible for emotion. She couldn't risk the disappointment that could come with getting her hopes up.

"Nobody should feel obligated to participate in this spell." Cassie forced herself to the edge of her chair. "I can't ask that of you, not when I've put you all through so much already."

Nick, Cassie noticed, had remained quiet during the whole discussion. She couldn't tell what he was thinking.

Melanie cleared her throat and raised her voice. "I believe this calls for a vote," she said, taking the center of the floor.

"All in favor," Melanie said, "raise your—"

"No!" Cassie called out. "I don't want there to be a vote. Whoever wants to do it should just show up. And whoever doesn't, no judgment."

She stood up too quickly and immediately felt dizzy. "Until then, I really need to go home. I'm sorry."

She traversed the room to the screen door and stepped down Diana's stone porch steps. No one chased after her. Even Adam had let her go.

~~~~~~~~~~~~~~~~

Cassie pushed open the front door to her house to find all the lights turned off. The interior of the old rooms seemed cavernous in the dark, and the wooden floorboards creaked with each step Cassie took to the stairs. She headed up the narrow flight, holding tight to the banister, until she reached her mother's bedroom door. Gently, she knuckled a soft knock.

A groggy voice replied, "Cassie?"

"Can we talk?" Cassie asked, turning the knob.

Her mother sat up. Cassie climbed into bed with her, deep into the folds of her warm, tangled sheets, as if she were a child. She couldn't remember the last time she'd actively sought her mother's affection this way.

Perhaps because she'd been woken from a sound sleep, her mother asked no questions, she only stroked Cassie's hair and listened.

Cassie explained everything that had happened as a result of destroying her father's book, how the Circle had defeated the ancestor spirits, but Cassie had lost her power in the process. She told her mother about the spell her friends were going to try.

"They want to offer me some of their power," Cassie said. "But it seems so impossible."

"The spell might not work," her mother clarified. "You understand that, don't you?"

Cassie did know that, but hearing it now, uttered so plainly from her mother's lips, brought tears to her eyes.

"There's a chance you might just be a regular girl from now on." Her mother's hand went still on the back of her head. "Normal."

That word sent a curious tingle up Cassie's spine. Such a loaded concept: *normal*.

"And it's a huge gesture for other witches to give up some of their power for you," her mother continued. "There's no more precious gift. Have you considered the possibility that it might not even be what you really want?"

Cassie pulled away from her mother to look her squarely in the eyes.

Her mother's face appeared honest and true. "I'm only saying that you shouldn't let your friends make this decision for you. You have to choose for yourself what you want your future to be. You're in a very unique position, Cassie, to be able to decide if you want magic or not. You didn't have that choice the first time."

Cassie returned her head to her mother's shoulder, and her mother resumed soothing her.

"Besides," her mother said, "if you're not truly open to accepting the power offered, no matter how hard everyone tries to give it to you, it'll have nowhere to go."

Cassie gave her mother's words some serious consideration. She thought about this past year. Since she had learned she was a witch, she'd often longed to be a normal girl again. She sometimes pitied herself for the complications that came with her magic.

But now, more than anything, she wished she'd appreciated her abilities more—and she hoped she could return to being the strong, powerful girl she'd grown into since she'd moved to New Salem.

Cassie had changed in the past year. She'd grown up. Being a witch *was* normal to her now, and there was no going back.

A regular life would never be enough anymore, even if it would be easier.

"I do want my power," Cassie said. She sat up straight and proud. "And I want to use those powers for good. To create change, to make a difference."

Her mother smiled. "Then I'll offer you all the power I can."

CHAPTER 28

Cassie woke up early to shower, and she already heard her mother moving around downstairs. They were equally anxious about the day before them, Cassie supposed. Anything could happen.

Cassie turned on the shower's tap to let the water heat up, then went to the mirror. She stared at herself as it began to fog over. Her face appeared the same as always. With power or without, she'd look the same to the outside world. But she felt different—hazy as the cloud over-running the mirror's surface. Until this moment Cassie hadn't really allowed herself to become too hopeful; the spell might not work. But as she slipped out of her pajamas and stepped into the steaming stream from her shower-head, she realized how much she wanted this.

She'd never wanted anything so badly in all her life.

But what if no one came?

Why hadn't she reacted better when her friends first proposed the idea of offering up their power? She'd showed them no appreciation at all. She practically threw a tantrum, getting up and walking out on them. It would be her own fault if her mother was the only one to join her at the ceremony today.

That thought trailed Cassie through the rest of her morning, right up to the moment she and her mother were approaching the beach.

From afar the sand looked like a white sheet with a few clusters of people standing upon it. Cassie couldn't make out any faces through the mist and fog. It might have been another group, some party or gathering of strangers. But as she inched closer she was overwhelmed by the sight that spread, clear and vivid, in front of her.

Faye was there, looking majestic with her dark dress blowing in the wind. Scarlett's hair shone red in the sun. Adam and Diana were helping everyone get organized. Her whole Circle had come. Max, who was standing close to Nick, gave him a nudge when he caught sight of Cassie and her mother approaching. Nick smiled warmly and waved.

Then Cassie began to look around more carefully. She saw Adam's grandmother, Mrs. Franklin, alongside Laurel's grandmother Quincey.

The crones came, she thought to herself. Her own grandmother wouldn't have believed it, to see these elders out in public fully prepared and willing to perform magic. Cassie said hello to each of them.

"Thank you for coming," she said, slightly breathless.

Adam's grandmother squeezed her hand. Her skin felt soft and wrinkled, so old. "I know you'll use my power well," she said.

"I promise to," Cassie answered.

Then Cassie noticed a tall, somewhat awkward man. It was Mr. Meade, Diana's father. He was standing beside a shorter man Cassie recognized as Suzan's father, Mr. Whittier. She hadn't seen him since his daughter's funeral.

Cassie greeted him, said thank you for coming, and then turned to her mother in disbelief. "You gathered the parents?"

Her mother modestly shrugged her shoulders. "All I did was go door to door and explain the situation. They decided for themselves to come."

If Cassie hadn't seen them with her own eyes she wouldn't have believed it. Chris and Doug were standing beside their nervous, long-limbed parents, who were known to be adamantly against magic. And Deborah's mom and dad, who had always denied ever being witches at all, were asking her to explain one more time how the spell would work.

Sean's father, slouching, beady-eyed Mr. Dulaney, who looked just like an older version of Sean, stood beside his son with his hand on Sean's bony shoulder. And if Cassie wasn't mistaken, Sean was leaning into his arm ever so slightly. His dad had come through for him. All of the parents had.

Even Faye's mom, Mrs. Chamberlain, an infamous recluse who never set foot out of bed, had come to the beach this morning. She was pale, lingering a bit apart from the others in a bulky gray sweatshirt that she clutched to her body like a cocoon—but she'd come.

Cassie jumped when a barking dog sprinted toward her. Even Raj had showed up on the beach for the spell. He sniffed his wet nose at her hands as Cassie giggled.

Adam chased after him, carrying a neon nylon leash. "He didn't want to miss out," he said, laughing.

There was a sparkle in Adam's blue-gray eyes, so much

like the sun glinting off the ocean. "Can you believe this turnout?" he said. "There's a lot of love for you on this beach right now, Cassie. I hope you can feel it."

Cassie's heart swelled within her chest. Adam was right. This crowd had assembled for her—all of this was just for *her*. The sight of all these friends, all these loved ones, suddenly brought tears to her eyes. She realized she had a much bigger family than she'd ever known.

~~~~~~~~~~

Cassie stepped to the center of the gigantic circle composed of every witch left in New Salem. Diana stood at the circle's northern point with her Book of Shadows in hand. She spoke in a loud, musical voice.

"Thank you for gathering here today," she said. "As the spell gets under way, each witch present must willingly offer Cassie a portion of his or her power, as a gift. You will get nothing in return. It has to be a completely selfless act."

Cassie looked around at all the willing faces, old, young, and in-between. Not one of them held her past against her, or her father's past against her. No one here today blamed her for being a *Blak*.

"Is everybody ready?" Diana asked.

A murmur of assent was all the prompting she needed.

"I'll go first," Diana announced and took a step forward, holding up a clear quartz crystal for everyone to observe.

Cassie stood perfectly still, open-handed. She cupped her palms as if she were trying to catch water from a fountain.

Diana ceremoniously placed the quartz in her open palms. She said, "I gift you this crystal, Cassandra Blake, as a symbol of my faith in you, and my allegiance to the community of witches, past, present, and future. Use this power well."

Her eyes radiated a shining love, for Cassie and for all who were present. Then she quietly returned to her place in the circle.

Adam was the next to step forward. He held up a vivid blue sapphire, then placed the stone beside Diana's in Cassie's open hands, repeating the same words: "I gift you this crystal, Cassandra Blake, as a symbol of my faith in you, and my allegiance to the community of witches, past, present, and future. Use this power well."

Adam kissed Cassie softly on the cheek before returning to his place in the circle.

Melanie offered Cassie pale green jade. Laurel gave her a majestically deep-hued amethyst. Deborah placed a yellow citrine into Cassie's hand that resembled the high morning sun. Suzan's father stepped forward holding up Suzan's favorite gemstone, an orange carnelian. Both of them had tears in their eyes when he offered it to Cassie.

Cassie's mother had brought her namesake stone, a color-changing alexandrite. She placed it on top of the crystal pile forming in Cassie's hands with a proud, loving smile.

There were twenty-one of them in all. One by one, each witch present stepped forward and made the offering.

Cassie's cupped hands filled with a pile of crystals like a multicolored glass mountain. In her palms lay pink danburite, translucent topaz, and precious tourmaline. There was silky tiger's eye and brassy pyrite; shimmering opal and speckled rainbow jasper. Their surfaces sparkled and felt cool upon her skin. The mass of them grew heavier with each stone, like a sinking, tipping scale.

Nick stepped forward holding up a hefty chunk of green selenite, which was a friendship stone with metaphysical properties. "Just knowing you," he whispered into her ear, "is enough for me. Seeing you every day, being there. I'll be your friend for life." He gave her a tender kiss on the forehead after placing the stone in her hands.

Cassie felt her heart brimming, abundant with love, spilling over.

Faye stepped to the center of the circle just after Nick. She offered Cassie her rare red star ruby. It was a grand gesture—the most powerful stone Faye owned—but she made no grandness of it. She gave Cassie a humble nod when she added it to the pile. "You deserve it," she said.

Scarlett was the only witch left who hadn't come forward. Cassie waited, her hands growing shaky now beneath the weight of all the stones. She could already feel their power charging through her, completing her. She was careful not to let a single one slip through her fingers.

Scarlett reached deep into her pocket and pulled out her offering. She held up a silvery black iron rose for everyone to admire. It was a variation of hematite, Cassie's and Scarlett's working crystal, with flat hexagonal edges clustered in a formation that resembled a flower. Its sheen reflected the sun like a mirror as she stepped forward. With both her hands, she placed it on the apex of the mountain of crystals in Cassie's palms.

Cassie felt her eyes widen as she took in the crystal's natural beauty. It was the perfect stone to top the pile, an exquisite gleaming rosebud. When Scarlett returned to her place in the circle, the offering was complete.

Cassie closed her eyes. The final recitation of the spell was hers to deliver.

She took a deep breath, allowing the power of all the crystals she held in her hands to fill her heart and soul.

She thought hard about the words on the brink of leaving her mouth. She had to mean them. She had to *feel* them. She had to be sure.

And she was.

"I am open to the power and love offered to me today," she said. "I accept it with unguarded gratitude."

She repeated those words three times, louder each time, and the moment the final consonant left her lips, the crystals heated in her hands—all of them together, as one. She suddenly became aware of the salt smell in the air and the splashing waves against the pier. She listened to it and felt her breathing slow. She could feel her own pulse and the pulse of the earth, and she became immersed in its rhythm. Then she felt a warmth flow from the stones, up her arms, through her heart, and out through the top of her head. She felt a light radiating from her pores. She was glowing.

She opened her eyes and looked around. She could see in the faces of her friends and loved ones that they also felt it. They, too, were flushed—not with the reception of power but by giving it freely. The whole group was radiant.

Cassie suddenly felt whole again, but without the darkness fighting her from inside. She felt part of the earth, and the sky, and the sea—she felt both tiny and vast all at once. The spell had worked. She felt like *Cassie*.

CHAPTER 29

Cassie reached for Adam's hand. "I love you so much," she said.

She looked down at their intertwined fingers, and it appeared: the silver cord, wrapping around their fingers and their hearts, roping their torsos like a lasso.

Adam rested his parted lips against her hair. "Always."

He kissed her on the mouth, and her whole body felt warm. She could feel the cord pulling them closer, humming and shimmering, more vibrant than ever.

A bright sun shined down on the vast blue water. Adam's eyes were wide and loving, and Cassie felt like she was collapsing into them as he looked at her. The moment was perfect.

With a swift motion, Adam swept her up into his arms. "I think we deserve a swim," he said.

"To the ocean!" Cassie called out for everyone to hear.

Nick raced for the tide. Chris, Doug, and Sean followed him. They ran knee-deep into the water, fully clothed.

Scarlett chased after Sean, diving for his head and dunking it underwater. Melanie, Laurel, and Deborah floated in up to their chins. Adam carried Cassie in deep enough for the sandy floor to dip down, and then shot ahead to join the game.

Max and Diana held one another close, treading water together. Cassie could see the filaments of their cord between them as they kissed the water droplets off each other's face.

Then Cassie noticed Faye, who was bobbing nearby, smiling sideways. Cassie grinned back at her, and Faye slapped a wave of water into her face.

Cassie caught the coming rush of saltwater right in her mouth, and Faye laughed aloud before she fled, kicking up more splashes through the surf behind her.

Cassie wiped the stinging wetness from her eyes. After everything they'd been through, Faye would continue being Faye—she wouldn't want her any other way.

The Circle drifted farther out into the horizon, chasing

and fleeing one another, spraying through the surf.

The dark times are over, Cassie thought. *At last.* She felt like she could float here, watching her friends like this, forever—her amazing and powerful friends, laughing and playing beneath the shining sun.

This was her destiny, and the things worth fighting for: friends, family, love.

Connection.

Why had she ever wanted to be anything other than what she was? A witch. With a Circle. Eternally linked to one another.

Cassie swam in toward the center of the action.

She was home, and she was herself. Everything was as it should be.

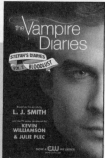
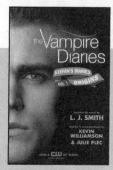
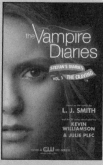

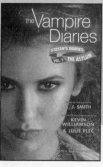
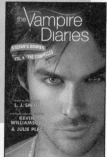

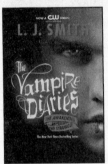

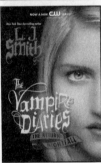
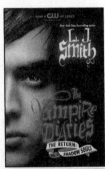
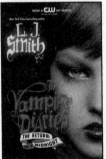
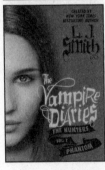
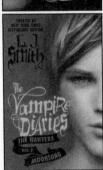

A THRILLING TALE OF
LOVE, WITCHCRAFT, AND THE SUPERNATURAL

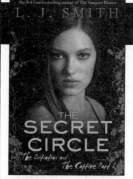

From the *New York Times* bestselling author of **The Vampire Diaries**

When Cassie moves to the small New England town of New Salem, she is lured into the most powerful and deadly in-crowd imaginable: the Secret Circle. The Circle always seems to get their way, and not just because they're popular; they're a coven of witches. The coven's power has controlled New Salem for centuries, and they initiate Cassie as one of their own. She soon learns that power comes at a price—and it's more dangerous than she knows.

Learn more at **jointhesecretcircle.com**

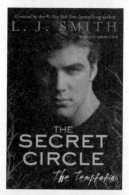

ALSO AVAILABLE!

The first book, now with art from the television show!